DRAGON RISING

DRAGON RISING

DRAGON APPARENT™ BOOK FOUR

TALIA BECKETT

DISRUPTIVE IMAGINATION®

This book is a work of fiction. All of the characters, organizations, and events portrayed in this novel are either products of the author's imagination or are used fictitiously. Sometimes both.

Copyright © 2022 Talia Beckett
Cover by Bandrei
Cover copyright © LMBPN Publishing

LMBPN Publishing supports the right to free expression and the value of copyright. The purpose of copyright is to encourage writers and artists to produce the creative works that enrich our culture.

The distribution of this book without permission is a theft of the author's intellectual property. If you would like permission to use material from the book (other than for review purposes), please contact support@lmbpn.com. Thank you for your support of the author's rights.

LMBPN Publishing
PMB 196, 2540 South Maryland Pkwy
Las Vegas, NV 89109

Version 1.00 January, 2023
eBook ISBN: 979-8-88541-779-2
Print ISBN: 979-8-88878-112-8

THE DRAGON RISING TEAM

Thanks to my JIT Team:

Zacc Pelter
Jeff Goode
Christopher Gilliard
Dorothy Lloyd
Diane L. Smith
Paul Westman
Jan Hunnicutt

DEDICATION

To Andrew.

Working with you on any story in any way is always fun, but you've made my 2022 a year to remember and helped me keep writing when I have struggled. I hope that 2023 is your year as much as possible. You deserve it.

At the beginning of my recent season of life you pointed out a hard truth to me. That no one was going to rescue me but myself. There was no knight in shining armor and I needed to slay those dragons and survive. Sure, people can help along the way, but I couldn't be the damsel in distress. It was hard to hear at the time but it was exactly the reminder I needed.

Consider me rescued.

— Talia

CHAPTER ONE

Walking into the royal tower was still a shock to my system. Everywhere was lavish. The furniture was ornate, the tower was one of the largest, and the suites were comfortable and bright.

Neritas and Flick, the two dragons who served as my self-appointed bodyguards, came in a fraction of a second later. They always flew behind me so no one could bombard me. Although I was now one of the most important dragons in the city, they were still worried that some of the dragons would be antagonistic.

In the past, I had been attacked while flying through a large storm cloud, though we had never seen who did it. No part of me wanted a repeat of that, but so far no one had made a similar attempt. Still, the atmosphere in the city had changed since I had proved my lineage and that I was the daughter of the previous king, and I wasn't sure it was for the better.

As my mother came out of her bedroom and smiled at me, I could at least focus on one thing I was grateful for.

Mom hadn't been in my life for long, but having her in it now had already made a difference.

"There you are. You're just in time. Several dragons are about to arrive to discuss what your coronation ceremony is going to look like over lunch." She smiled briefly before motioning for me to take a seat on a large dining chair at the far end of the room.

Still mentally processing what she had told me, I walked over and sat. If nothing else, I was hungry, and the constant supply of food coming up to the place wasn't something to ignore. I enjoyed getting treated like royalty in some ways, and I wouldn't deny it.

In other ways I didn't. There had been a lot of meetings with a lot of people who wanted to tell me how I should act and what I should do. It was weird. Mostly I just wanted to hang out with my family and friends and make sure the gate restraining the biggest evil in the world didn't break. I'd barely had the chance to talk to my mom alone, let alone work out how to unite the dragons around the world to power the gate.

Neritas and Flick followed, drawn by the promise of food. It was almost comical as they picked at bits of food they didn't think anyone would notice missing. I rolled my eyes as Ben also appeared and joined us.

Having the four of them with me felt like my family was all together. Ben had become a sort of father figure to me since Anthony had died, and more so since Mom had confirmed that my biological father was also dead. It was all strange and new in some ways, but also familiar.

Given how big the tower was and how many bedrooms there were, Neritas and Flick had also moved in. Neritas had no family of his own, and Flick didn't get along well with his father. It was better for both of them—at least that was what I told myself. Mom had commented that I needed to be careful about any romantic interests they might have.

I was a red dragon, and only red dragons could power the gate, apparently. That meant any partner I considered in life would have to be red. There was one problem with that restriction: as far as we were aware, there weren't any other red dragons. At least none in the neighboring dragon cities.

Others might be lingering in the human world and trying to hide, or in cities in other countries, from where there was less communication. Because of the secrecy of the dragon community, there were pockets of them around the world, and they could have all sorts living among them. I hoped that if there were other red dragons, they would be received better than I had been.

We were still waiting several minutes later, and I was considering stealing some of the food. It was getting cold. I picked up a shrimp from a small pile in sauce on top of a pastry cup and slipped it into my mouth just as our guests arrived.

It was exactly the worst timing, and I froze with my fingers in my mouth for a moment before pulling them out. As an assistant came over to the table and my mom got up again to usher them toward us, I tried to chew surreptitiously while I stood. The etiquette of what to do in this sort of situation was new to me, but I tried to make the best of it. I wiped my fingers on the side of my pants while they greeted my mom and companions.

Finally, they turned to me, and Griffin bowed. I raised an eyebrow, not having expected the gesture. I wasn't the queen yet, and I wasn't trying to lord it over anyone.

"Please, don't." I motioned for him to stop.

Griffin rose again but smiled as he studied me.

"Not the kind to stand on ceremony?" he asked as he straightened his back.

"No. I just want to do what's needed and protect this planet."

"Then let's get you crowned and help you do that. After all, it's in our best interests, isn't it?"

Appreciating the eagerness he was displaying and ready to get this whole coronation charade over and done with, I sat back down.

This was signal enough to Flick, Neritas, and Mom to start eating, and I offered some of the platters and dishes to our guests and tucked in myself.

Thankfully Griffin seemed to understand that we were all hungry, and he didn't steal our focus from the food too much at first. He stuck to topics like the weather and how everyone liked the apartments we were in.

I appreciated that he engaged Mom on certain subjects, asking her if she was happy enough in the city and apologizing for the lack of land.

"I can see the sense in having a city on the water when shadow catchers find it so toxic in such large amounts. With it holding the seat of power for our kind, I am sure that there is a good deal of sense in its location. And it is beautiful in its own way. I have missed it."

"You used to live here?"

"I visited when I was much younger and the king was

still alive. As his guest, though rarely to the liking of everyone here."

Although I appeared as if I was focused on my food, I listened closely to everything Griffin and my mother were saying, wondering if it impacted how my mom felt now that she was back. She had returned to the city with me without much complaint, but she hadn't mentioned being here before, either.

Had I once again neglected to notice the pain and discomfort of those around me? It was sobering and reminded me that being in charge involved a lot more than pursuing a single agenda. The dragons around me were making sacrifices to support me and help achieve that goal, and I needed to be aware of it and make sacrifices in return.

When I thought of what this was doing to everyone around me, I had to wonder whether it was worth it. While saving the world was necessary, I knew that being queen was less so. They weren't completely linked.

Mom was being deliberately vague about her life when Griffin asked if she'd liked it here, and it created an awkward moment I tried to rescue.

"I'm sure you haven't come all the way to the top of this tower to talk of the merit of land dwelling versus water. Why don't we begin going over the process you have so far?" I hoped it wouldn't sound dismissive of a way of life that my mother might appreciate more than this. Thankfully she exhaled with what appeared to be relief and her body relaxed again when Griffin turned to me.

"Yes, of course. I imagine you have a lot to do today. And I don't have a small amount either." Griffin opened a folder in front of him and showed me a crude map of the city showing the towers and the small chunk of land that connected us to the coast north of LA. Markings and lines were already drawn.

"I thought it would be fitting for you to begin from here and end in the elders' chambers, where there is the biggest opportunity for an audience. In between, there are several markers and elements that will give the crowds something to see and probably record, take photos, that sort of thing."

As Griffin spoke and pointed at some of the more heavily marked elements of his drawing, my frown deepened. This wasn't the sort of ceremony I had been thinking of. When I'd been asked for my input, I had asked to just get the crown and get on with making sure Earth was safe.

Now there was talk of a full-on crowning ceremony, complete with fly-bys, a feast, and all sorts of time-consuming and unnecessary elements.

"I think that all might be a bit much." It was the kind of thing that was going to take most of the day, involve multiple outfits, and be more like a wedding day than a simple put-a-crown-on-my-head—a crown I already owned and could wear—ceremony before getting on with the task of fixing the gate.

Griffin looked at me as if he was trying to work out what I could mean.

"I appreciate the effort that you've gone to in thinking of all these things," I added, not wanting to offend him. "But I don't need a big ceremony. And I don't think getting me to do a big speech or toast is a great idea. Neither is asking someone like me to lead some kind of special flying display."

"I'll admit, this got bigger as the other elders and the royal staff talked it over. There hasn't been a coronation in a very long time and we're all quite excited, but I can see how it would seem overwhelming. We can get someone to help you write a speech, and we can keep the flying limited and allow it to be choreographed well enough that you can peel off and land before it's done."

As Griffin spoke, more despair filled me. It was clear that he was trying to be nice, but he wasn't understanding my objections. Nor did he seem to understand the level of animosity between me and others in the city. Proving I was queen hadn't made as much of a difference as I'd hoped.

It didn't help that one or two of the elders weren't satisfied with my proof. It seemed that a birth certificate, a mother who confirmed it, and witnesses to my powers, which only royal red dragons had, wasn't enough.

I had no other way of proving my lineage, though. To some degree, I was also taking the word of my mother and everyone around me as proof that I was who I thought I was.

It could be a lie, but if so, it was an elaborate one. On top of that, some weird stone dais on a hidden island in a lake somewhere had given me its blessing. I knew that the past dragons and the power they had given me was the best proof I could have. But that was harder to show than anything else.

While I felt a connection still to the island and could have found my way back to it blindfolded if I needed to, I couldn't show anyone else that feeling. My doubt was gone, but I couldn't remove the doubts of others.

Over the course of the next hour, I did my best to get

Griffin to understand that I didn't need or want to show off. Unhelpfully, Neritas and Flick encouraged it—Flick thought I should demonstrate how much better I could fly than everyone else, and Neritas thought they needed to be reminded that I was powerful and had enough respect to be made a fuss of. Almost as if I was daring anyone to challenge the power and strength I was showing.

Despite their points of view, I knew that I couldn't be arrogant about all this. I had to get more people to like me. Lording my status over them wasn't going to win hearts.

When Griffin left, I sighed and watched him fly down to the elders' tower, a couple of levels below the main chamber. It wasn't too far down, but there were almost no other towers in the city as tall as this one, and for a moment I stayed to enjoy the view and think.

My mother came to my side.

"Sometimes being royalty is a fine balancing act of showing people that you are in charge but also giving them something normal to relate to. Some want you on a pedestal so they can have faith that you'll make better decisions. Some get comfort from knowing that you're just like them."

"And somehow I have to be both at once."

"Not at once. Just often enough that each sees what they want to see. Humans and dragons alike have a remarkable ability to latch on to what makes them feel good and ignore that which makes them uncomfortable." I heard the tiredness in my mother's voice and knew she didn't say the words with disdain for the issue or the people she was referring to, but more of a resigned acceptance.

"None of this is anything I ever expected to have to do."

I knew I was pitying myself and not sure I liked it, but also not sure of the way out yet.

"I'm sorry. There was no way to protect you and to raise you with the knowledge of who you were or with anyone to prepare you from a young age. Anthony was doing what he could, and Ben has done a remarkable job when he had no idea what he was preparing you for, but it's not the same as being nurtured toward this."

"Yet here I am."

"You will do what you need to, and the planet will be safe. Would you like me to help you write your speech?" Mom smiled as she tucked a stray lock of hair back behind my ear.

I nodded, grateful for anything that meant we could spend more time together and grateful that I would have her experience to guide me. She may not have been a royal figure, but she had been the partner of one. Of everyone left alive, she was the most qualified to teach me what I needed to know.

CHAPTER TWO

The day I was meant to be crowned came ever closer. It was less than a week now, and almost everything had been decided and put into place. I was left with the task of rehearsing and trying to make it as smooth as possible. I wasn't involved in every facet of this great event, but I had Jared helping with the flying part and, as always, Flick and Neritas had been chosen to fly with me.

They were excited and grateful that they'd been included, although Neritas didn't appreciate that he had been asked to wear something other than the scruffy, ripped jeans and long leather jacket he normally sported. They'd suggested a suit, but a compromise had been found, with a shorter, smarter-looking leather jacket and not a rip in sight.

I grinned as I thought about it and followed Jared toward our next landing point. He was running us slowly through the elements of the day and all the flying I would need to do. There were six black dragons with me acting as my honor guard until I chose the full team myself.

Of course, I planned to get Alitas, Merrik, and Cios back, as well as Reijo, but for now Reijo had been asked to fly with Ben and my mother, the two blue dragons accompanying the red dragon and ensuring her safety.

Although no one had been rude to my mother and she had been able to move about the city as she wished, I got the feeling that it hadn't been easy for her either. I didn't want her to feel left out or unappreciated—or worse, vulnerable and scared.

Jared beamed at me as we landed on an open tower between the flying tower and the small section of land at the base of the city.

"And then we'll pause here for a moment as your mother, Ben, and Reijo land on the other tower, doing a similar though slightly shorter fly-by. Another couple of black guards will be with them, and I believe Capricia—"

"Capricia isn't part of the fly-by," a guard interrupted Jared.

This seemed to surprise Jared as much as me.

"Oh, I thought she would, as captain of the guard and a white dragon."

"I don't know her reasons, but she declined to be involved." The guard made it sound as if Capricia's reasons were as bad as I feared, but I did my best to hide my reaction. I might be jumping to the wrong conclusions. She was the captain of the city guard. In an event like this, she would have lots of responsibilities, not just the expectation that she might want to fly with me or my mother.

Making a mental note to ask if she was okay with everything the next time I saw her, I refocused on Jared and his description of what would come next. Because I could fly well, they were getting me to show off a little, and a couple of the tricks we were going to attempt needed some practice.

After a description of what to do next from Jared, we all dove off the tower again. I transformed within a fraction of a second and spread my wings. It felt good and was one of my favorite things about discovering my true heritage. I was a dragon, and nothing felt as good as flying around the city.

It had taken me a few days to get the hang of flying, but a lot longer to grasp how to transform smoothly. Now, thanks to a natural boost from my ancestors and connecting to them and their memories a week earlier, I could do both with ease.

Doing the moves I'd been asked to do was easy. None of it was as challenging as the flying we were doing in our advanced lessons. I was mostly doing all this for show and to make an entrance, it seemed. I had no idea why, but Mom had told me to go with it, and I wasn't going to make too much of a fuss about this part.

When I was still several hundred yards away from the strip of land that contained a small parking lot, a guard station, and an area of road that connected to the mainland, I noticed a shadow appear in front of me.

Possible trouble, Neritas warned in my head.

Before I could do more than look up and realize they were flying by the sun and so were almost invisible, they were swooping down at me.

I banked to the side, trying to avoid being hit, but another dragon appeared from around the tower.

The pair of them forced me down as I heard Jared roar

a warning. Almost immediately, the black dragons that had been flying with me caught up and flanked me, forming a circle with Jared in front and Neritas and Flick adding extra protection above me.

Normally this was more than enough to dissuade anyone from bothering me, but today more dragons appeared, and they kept diving toward us, trying to scare the group off our path. It ruined the practice despite Jared roaring several more times at them.

He guided us to land, bumping into a green dragon and a white dragon who persistently blocked the way. When we were close to landing and another green dragon flew in front of us and got in the way, I roared my anger as well.

Finally, we got close enough to land and transform. I hesitated, but I was used to fighting in human form and my instinct of self-preservation took over. Neritas and Flick landed at my sides. The dragons flew away as others came closer, still in dragon form and out of sight until the last possible moment.

I ducked as claws narrowly missed me, and Jared yelled for more guards.

None came as the dragons all banked. I was wearing the sword and shield that Neritas had found for me, so I raised the shield, drew on the magic of the myriad of dragons around me, including my attackers, and formed a barrier around all of us where we stood on the ground.

When the next dragon flew at me, I raised the shield and walked right toward them.

"Scarlet, what are you doing?" Jared asked, fear clear in his voice.

He got his answer when a green dragon flew straight

for me and I simply stood there, bracing the shield between me and the dragon's claws. More city dwellers yelled and ran over, probably thinking I was about to be clawed, but the dragon only hit the shield. A shock wave ran through me, but the equipment I had held me firm.

The dragon let out a pained roar and almost fell from the sky, both wings down and beating either side of me as it fought to get up and away from what was causing it pain.

I stood my ground as another followed, trying to get to me or my friends as well.

"Nice! It works on them too," Flick yelled, sounding delighted as he came in closer behind me.

Although I wasn't happy about hurting other dragons, I was grateful it worked and that I could protect myself and the dragons around me.

"Come in close to me," I told Jared and the black dragons he had appointed to guard me.

None of them needed any encouragement as another dragon tried to get at me. They snapped with their mouth, coming closer to landing. Again, I shoved the powered-up shield toward them, keeping the sword sheathed so no one could accuse me of doing anything but defending myself and holding my ground.

The dragon's tooth caught the shield and it broke off, clattering to the ground as the dragon bellowed and flinched. It gave me another shockwave, but magic helped me stand still as before.

I glanced around to check that all my friends and guards were with me and safe. Everyone but Flick and Neritas was wide eyed and either staring at me and the shield or the dragons I'd hurt. Two of them were yelling in pain, which finally deterred the rest from attacking me, and they all peeled off to land in towers nearby. None of them took human form as they sat watching me.

Slowly, I turned and lowered the shield, sure the threat was over, if only temporarily. So many of the faces looking back at me were filled with shock, wide eyed and staring.

"I know that many of you don't like me, or the idea of me being royalty. I get that. I'm not sure I like the idea either. But I've done nothing to deserve being attacked, and the dragons with me especially don't deserve your anger or aggression. I don't want to hurt any of you, but I have the same rights as any other dragon to be in this city and I will defend myself and my friends if I have to."

No one replied, but Capricia finally appeared, morphing into human form as her white dragon shape landed.

"Stand down." Capricia didn't sound particularly bothered by having her queen attacked in the city she was responsible for.

I raised my eyebrows as Ben landed, as well as Brenta, Griffin, and several more black dragon guards.

Brenta strode toward me. "This is not acceptable behavior."

"I don't know. I think Scarlet just saved me from having my head scalped by Verity." Jared came to my side and glared at the elder.

This made the older woman stop in her tracks and look around.

"We were doing our practice with Jared and several dragons came at us out of nowhere." Neritas stepped forward as well, raising his voice so others could hear us.

"If Scarlet hadn't used her powers and channeled our magic to defend us, this would have got ugly."

"I don't think we need to be as concerned or worried as that. You're all fine." Brenta raised her chin, trying to look as if she was in control.

"I'm surprised it even got as far as it did so close to the main guard center. You took a long time to respond, Capricia. I think that concerns me most, given it's your job to protect us all, not Scarlet's," Neritas shot back.

"Are you suggesting something, Neritas?" Capricia asked.

Griffin stepped and put a hand on the captain of the guard's shoulder. She glared at Neritas a moment longer before flicking her gaze to me. I'd have expected her look to grow gentler as she did, but if anything, it grew fiercer before she turned and stalked off.

After declaring that I was the rightful heir to the throne, I had expected some resistance and general dislike of it, but I hadn't expected it to be quite as bad as this.

I was aware that there were still a lot of people staring at me and no one had done anything to reprimand the dragons who had attacked me. They had not gone to help them either, though, and one of them had lost teeth.

"I think we should escort you back to your apartment." Jared spoke barely above a whisper as he leaned in closer.

I agreed. The tension was clear, and I wasn't sure which way it would go.

Within seconds we were all back in the air and in dragon form. This time everyone hung back, and several dragons landed or got out of our way so we had clear skies ahead of us. As they did, I wondered how many of them were moving out of fear or because they wanted to make things easier for me.

As I landed, I saw Mom, her body shaking as she stood by a window. I got the feeling that she had seen or felt the entire thing. When I was inside the building enough that few others would have been able to see me, she rushed over and gave me a hug.

For a moment, I appreciated the affection. The city had been tense before, but I'd never been attacked so openly. This place had been safety from the shadow catchers. A bit like the homes I had grown up in—not perfect, but fundamentally safe enough. I got the feeling that was no longer true.

As I pulled back, Mom searched my face and looked me over.

"I'm okay," I assured her. "Shaken, but not harmed."

Before she could respond, more dragons joined us, most of the elders appearing and coming inside as well. All of them were serious, and I got the impression that I wasn't in their best graces.

Ben stepped forward, stopping Brenta from speaking.

"I think you have all heard about what's just happened. Please give Scarlet a moment for us to check that she's okay, administer aid, and then we will all come to the chambers to discuss this and what should be done about it."

Brenta's eyes narrowed, but Griffin and several of the other elders turned to leave, and it gave her little choice but to go as well.

"Don't take too long. I have two dragons in the chamber who have informed me that they were severely injured by Scarlet, and I wish to understand these events."

"I'm just as interested in resolving this, I assure you." I couldn't keep the iciness from my tone. This was bullshit, and I was getting antagonism yet again because of who I'd been born as. Dragons of my color were required to keep the world alive, and it made no sense for the other dragons to be so angry at red dragons.

No one spoke until only Neritas, Flick, Ben, and Mom were left with me. Immediately Mom hugged me again.

"I'm sorry that this is happening to you. I had hoped that the dragons would be more accepting of red dragons if they were given some time without them. I had no idea that they would start teaching that we weren't even needed anymore and that the gate was safe."

"It's not your fault. None of them realize how much danger the world is in. It's as if they have all forgotten or been taught that everything is fine. They literally have no clue that they need me."

"I'm pretty sure that telling them isn't going to get us anywhere either. They won't want to believe us." Ben took my hand. "But I meant what I said a moment ago. Are you okay? That looked nasty."

I nodded, trying to work out what to say. Already I felt awful for what I had done. Without hesitation, I had pulled on the magic of all the dragons around me, including those who had attacked. And without their permission. It was different when I had a group and was asking them to trust me to defeat a shadow catcher or protect others. But I had used the magic of enemy dragons to make me strong enough to hurt them. I was feeling defeated already and with no idea of what I should do other than face the wrath of the elders and work out how to get them to defend me so I didn't have to. Capricia's reaction had been difficult and unexpected. She'd stood beside me in battle and been to the island that had confirmed that I was who I said I was. Surely she should have been more supportive?

Either way, all I was doing staying in my tower was delaying the inevitable conversation. I had to go before the elders and see if I could sort this out.

CHAPTER THREE

Although flying was dangerous, the elders' tower was close enough below the tower I lived in that I took the risk and dove for the entrance in dragon form. I could glide, and for a brief second, I was okay again and the weight of the world wasn't on my shoulders.

As I landed, I took in the number of dragons already in the chambers. There were several, all in human form. Two of them were clearly injured. One girl I recognized as a green dragon who liked to keep her form part human and part dragon. She cried quietly. Two of her teeth were missing and her face was a mess of cuts, swelling and bruises. The other wasn't someone I recognized but she clutched her arm to her chest, a scarf around it like a makeshift sling.

I looked them over, but I didn't feel much sympathy. It was like seeing a bully who lost a fight because they underestimated the strength of the kid they thought was easy meat. They had thought me easy prey and found I wasn't. If

I hadn't defended myself, I would look the same or worse right now.

Both of them glared at me. I didn't blame them. Hurting them when they had intended to hurt me wasn't going to make them like me any more than they already did.

Capricia also stood in the chamber, along with everyone who had been flying with me and about ten other citizens I vaguely recognized. Some of them looked at me with sympathy, others more curiosity, and the rest openly hostile.

"I'm sorry to keep you all waiting," I said, using my magic to reach for the artifact in the center of the room that would let me know who within the chambers was telling the truth.

If the other elders detected me doing so, none of them said anything or let on. I felt all of their minds as they used it, all of them present and making sure that they were able to feel the emotion of everyone inside.

Being connected to it also helped me get a better read on the room. Everyone felt a little differently, but the amount of fear mixed with anger surprised me. Both the dragons I'd hurt were terrified.

"And I'm sorry for hurting you both. I have an artifact in my chambers that will help take away the pain and aid your healing if you'll allow me to have it fetched. I think it would be far kinder to both of you to do that before anything else."

A silence followed my words, but Flick gave me a nod and headed off to get the artifact I spoke of. He'd seen me use it in the past and had been there when my mother had given it to me. He was also one of the few dragons whom I felt I could trust with my belongings. That I didn't have to ask also meant the two dragons didn't have to reply.

With that in progress, I felt farther out and noticed that Capricia felt a lot of anger as well. Given she was responsible for the city and everyone in it, there were a lot of reasons she might feel that emotion, and I didn't know what I could do to help her yet. The rest had calmed with my offer of healing and the calm I was trying to project. I wasn't a white dragon and able to influence the emotions of others in the same way, but it was a start.

Flick was swift, and I took the device from him.

"Can I draw from you four?" I asked my closest companions.

"Of course." Neritas nodded as all four of them came closer.

Aware I had an audience for what would appear to be a strange act, possibly something they also feared, I moved slowly. The girl with her arm in a sling moved back as I came closer, but the other one was too upset and clearly in pain.

I started to heal her, channeling the magic of my friends and myself into the artifact and moving it near enough to the damaged areas that it could reach out with a golden light and begin to heal.

Her eyes went wide as she started to relax, and the worst of the damage slowly grew better and the swelling on her face went down. Although it wasn't perfect and only aided the body in doing what it could naturally do anyway, it was enough that everyone in the room could see the difference by the time I was done.

Her friend was less shy after seeing the artifact in

action, and before long she removed the scarf and flexed a hand.

"You'll need to both be careful for a while, but if you give it a day or so, I can do some more again." I nodded at them and handed the artifact back to Flick for safekeeping.

"Well, that's a useful trick and make no mistake," Griffin said. "I know that others have said that it was possible in their accounts of you leaving the city, but seeing it in use is quite another matter."

"That might be so, but we need to discuss what happened to cause those injuries." Brenta sounded far less in awe of what I had done.

A part of me wanted to tell her she was fired for being so clearly biased, but I couldn't do that. Not yet anyway. And I didn't think it would win anyone over if I did.

"I'd like to begin." Jared stepped forward while I was opening my mouth to tell Brenta I'd been attacked and throw in some snark to go with it.

"Go ahead. Your understanding of events would be valued," Griffin replied, but Brenta shot him a look and I got the impression that the elders weren't unanimous on that particular decision.

Jared talked about running through the preparation of the coronation with me and how Neritas had spotted danger and several dragons getting too close. Jared proved that he knew the entire city by naming each dragon who had forced me to land and explaining how he knew it was them. He described how I had taken human form and the dragons had kept coming. There were gasps from Griffin and a couple of the other elders, but Jared only paused a moment before finishing his description of events from his point of view.

The part that interested me the most, however, was his account of what I did to defend us.

"Then I felt a pull on the magic inside of me. As if something was drawing it gently toward a task I'd had no idea I could do. I felt it go toward Scarlet and the shield she carried. A barrier formed that protected us all as more dragons came hurtling in. Scarlet used magic to save us and seemed just as shocked as these two young women when it hurt them and almost knocked Scarlet off her feet."

I felt for the reaction of the room. Jared was clearly telling the truth, and they would all know that, but I was still feeling anger from Brenta, and it seemed to worsen at this description, not improve.

"If I understand previous accounts of Scarlet's correctly, this use of magic is not new?" Brenta was talking about me as if I wasn't there, but glaring at me as if she expected me to answer the question.

"It's not new," I replied, but stopped as soon as I felt her anger grow again. What was I missing about their reaction? Did they not realize it was an accident? "But I had no idea it would do harm. It was meant to just defend me and my friends from an attack."

"But you've used it to kill shadow catchers." Brenta's voice was loud, and she looked fidgety and agitated, she was so angry.

"Not directly. The sword kills them, and I didn't use that. I think the shield is more broad than a direct attack and defends by repelling the demons. I would never use the sword on another dragon." I felt the room slipping away despite my words. They didn't understand why I'd done it.

Glancing at my friends, I felt the warmth from them.

"My intention was only to protect myself and those with me," I added a moment later.

Brenta's anger grew another notch. "But you couldn't be sure about what you were doing." In some ways it was justified.

"We were in human form and vulnerable, and dragons in this city were attacking us, and you're angry at Scarlet for defending us the only way she knew how?" Neritas strode forward, his long leather coat billowing out behind him. "What kind of elder are you that you are angry at the victim of an attack?"

"She's not harmed. She's never harmed," Capricia countered, also moving forward. "Everything she does she draws on the strength of others to do, like a parasite, just like the red dragons before her."

I didn't know what to do or say as Ben chimed in, then some of the guard, everyone hurling accusations and anger in attack or defense of my actions. Looking around, I felt the anger rising but everyone was in some way telling the truth. They believed what they were saying and genuinely felt concern. There was no arguing with people who were seeing something from a different point of view like this, and no one seemed to be able to stop it.

Taking a deep breath, I tried to calm myself. I wanted to yell and rant and be angry that I had been threatened by my own kind, but it wouldn't help. It was my job, before anything else, to unite these creatures and power the gate, and that meant I couldn't be a hotheaded red dragon. I had to be better than that.

"Please, all of you, stop," I said as loudly as I dared. "What is done cannot be undone. I thought my actions would cause no harm. They clearly did, and I have done what I can to put it right. While I should have been more careful, I also should never have been attacked, and neither should anyone else. You're all right and you all have a point. Tempers and anger will not lead this city forward."

The room took a moment to become completely quiet, but I knew they had all heard me. It was almost crazy to think of me being the calm one, but I realized that the atmosphere was being influenced and the anger fueled. Capricia was making it worse.

Hoping that she was doing it unconsciously, I went to her side.

"You are one of the most important dragons in this city and it has been an honor to fight beside you. I hear what you are saying, but you need to let go of anger as well and talk this over rationally," I said far more quietly as I put a hand on her shoulder.

"I have nothing more to say to you. You're reckless and not my queen."

Before I could say anything else, Capricia growled and strode from the chamber. Several of the guards went with her, along with the two injured dragons. I watched them go, clueless about how to fix this and make them understand that I didn't want this any more than they did.

"I think this is one of those unfortunate events that should be avoided in the future. Scarlet, would you be willing to leave the sword and shield in your rooms when in the city?" Griffin asked, his tone far gentler than anyone's had been in some time.

"Absolutely not," Mom replied before I could do more than instinctively reach for the shield I had slung on my back.

"If Scarlet leaves her shield in her room, what would she do if dragons attack her again, as they have today? She's about to become queen. There was a time when dragons faced the death penalty for attacking a royal."

"She's not queen yet," Brenta pointed out. "And not innocent, nor necessarily the best dragon to lead us. Already we have had to try to hush up her incidents on several occasions, and this last video of all of you fighting has been the hardest to bury yet."

I finally lost my temper with the elder. "What was I meant to do, then, let them kill me and everyone else? Do you want me dead?" She was entirely impossible, and if she would stop sowing dissent and encouraging disdain for me and instead focus on the bigger picture, we might stand a chance.

"I wouldn't wish death upon anyone, especially not by a shadow catcher, but this city has been ruled by the elders for many years and was flourishing. Trouble follows you and your entire family line, and not everyone wants it."

"Some would argue that trouble only follows her because her authority and power as the royal red isn't respected as it should be," Griffin shot back, surprising me. "Be careful what you say, Brenta, to your future queen. There's disagreement and opinions, and there's judgment clouded by the long-held power of our positions, and you are close to straying from the former to the latter."

After another awkward silence, an elder chipped in to yet another argument over what constituted respect, whether they were convinced I was the heir, and what should be done about my sword and shield.

My mother came to me with a sad expression on her face. Almost all of us were being ignored except for Neritas, who also joined the argument. He was fiercely disagreeing with Brenta and leaving Griffin to argue with another elder.

I had no clue what to do, but this couldn't go on.

As my mother took my hand, she leaned in.

"You have my support no matter what happens and what you do. Do what feels right in your heart and trust yourself."

The words made me panic more at first. How would I know what the right thing to do was? How would I know what would unite all these dragons? They were so fixated on whether I would make a good queen and whether the people liked me or not that I couldn't get anyone to focus on what truly mattered: getting the gate powered.

"Enough!" I yelled as loudly as I could, realizing what I needed to do.

A stunned silence ensued, and I was pretty sure most of the elders only stopped because they weren't used to being yelled at. I made my way to the center of the room and raised my shield.

"What matters to me most is not that I am queen, but that the dragon community is united. I am not like the red dragons before me. I do not desire power. But I do have a gift that can be used to protect the dragons of this city."

Brenta went to interrupt me again, but I made the

shield I was carrying flash slightly and she shut her mouth again so hard that it audibly clicked.

"With all this in mind, I hereby withdraw my claim to the dragon throne. I may be descended from a king, but I cannot force a nation of people who don't want a queen to accept one."

No one spoke. Their arms fell to their sides as they forgot their arguments. No one had expected this.

CHAPTER FOUR

Ben was the first to speak, and seemed to be in complete shock. "You can't."

"I need to," I replied as the elders got up off their chairs and came down to me.

"No. You need to be in charge and stop this city from falling apart." Neritas narrowed his eyes and I feared that he was going to stalk away, but I went to him and put my hand on his shoulder.

"I know that you want a queen, and I am constantly grateful for the support you have given me and faith you have that I will be good for the dragons of this world, but I can't do this when it is causing so many arguments in a place like this, where everyone is meant to be calm and relatively impartial."

"You can't know which is better in the long term." Neritas relaxed despite his response and it made me feel a little better about my resolve not to demand a throne that wasn't being offered to me.

"I can't, for sure. But I do know that my conscience

wouldn't live with me being the reason that this community divides itself. This is my choice. Can you respect the decision I've made and help me unite us all instead?"

He nodded and stepped back, and it took the desire to push me to be queen out of everyone else as well. My mother still held my hand, and she gave it a squeeze as everyone else shifted and I was left looking at Brenta.

"This isn't what I expected either, but I won't deny that I think it's for the best. This city doesn't need a dragon on the throne."

"That it might not, but everything else I have spoken here today I still agree with. Your anger that I defended myself in what would have been a brutal attack had I not prevented it is telling of your character. No victim of any kind should ever be made to feel guilty for trying to prevent their own harm. I humbly suggest that you learn to have more empathy for those in need. It will serve you well as an elder of this city."

Brenta bristled and raised her chin. I expected her to say something, but she simply glared at me and returned to her seat.

I exhaled as the other elders stayed where they were. Griffin came up to me next.

"I'm proud of you. Given the situation, you've done a very brave and selfless thing, and by doing that alone you've proved to me that I was right to think well of you as a dragon and as a leader. I would like to recommend you be given the option of councilor, and then the career progression for an elder will be open to you in future. You have shown yourself to be a valuable asset to this community and city and have a great magic running through your veins. You need to be part of our group and bring your voice to these chambers on a regular basis."

"I would love to." It could only be good for the city to have more elders in general. "In the meantime, I suggest my mother be an elder. She's got many tales of old, and wisdom passed to her from the royal lines. She could also serve the city well."

It was a bit of a long shot, given that I hadn't asked my mother if she was okay with being volunteered, but it allowed us to put someone on the elders' circle right away who could help me unite the people of the city and undo some of the damage again.

More discussion erupted around me, and Brenta once again objected.

"If I allow this, where will it end? Are we just trading one kind of leader for the same one with a different name?" Brenta crossed her arms.

"And if we don't allow this, what do you think all the disillusioned youth and dragons who want her as a queen will do?" Ben asked.

"It's a good question and something we should consider when we take this news to the rest of the city," Griffin replied.

The more I encountered and talked to the bubbly elder, the more I liked Griffin. He wasn't too argumentative most of the time, but he was clear about his opinions. And he thought of others and of points of view I hadn't considered. Most importantly, he also wanted to unite the city. He could get heated, but none of us had stayed out of this argument or refrained from throwing barbs this time.

"I'd like to see some calm return to the city, and for the

tension to leave," another of the elders added. She returned to her chair, which encouraged them all to do the same. I stood in the middle of the chamber with Neritas, Flick, Mom, Jared, and Ben, and some space to calm as well. The black guards who had remained kept a respectful distance, but I saw they were also looking a lot more relaxed, and no one was standing with shields raised anymore.

With the pressure of being a queen and having to lead gone from my shoulders now, I felt better already. It was strange to know I had given it up entirely. For almost the entire time I had known I was a dragon, I had also tried to prove I was a royal descendant. Part of me had done it to increase my safety, but it had come at a high cost.

Thinking about what I was giving up wasn't hard. For now, at least, this was the right course of action.

"I think everyone in this room can agree that the city needs to calm down and needs to be given time to recover," Brenta said, looking anywhere but at me. "Let us discuss everything this entails and possible appointments of other positions one at a time, and if need be, come back tomorrow."

"This is a good idea but there are definitely some areas that need to be considered in the light of this revelation that must be done today and done well," Griffin responded, and others nodded along with him. "I wouldn't normally invite others to the rooms where we eat and deliberate, but given the nature of these events and the people in this chamber with us, I believe we should all go there now and eat together and try to come up with a solution that satisfies everyone and keeps our citizens safest."

I thought Brenta might disagree with this at first, but

she didn't, instead nodding her consent. More than a little intrigued and definitely ready to eat, I hoped this meant I could stuff my face with food. Being so tense and worried about being a good leader had impacted my appetite, and I was suddenly ravenous.

While I knew that the city was dangerous for me still and I wasn't going to magically get along with everyone, I knew that it was likely to go back to a level of animosity that I could tolerate. People being aggressive and actively trying to hurt me was different from them making verbal jibes or giving me the silent treatment. I could cope with the latter.

The elders led the way as we emerged from the chambers. Instantly, I noticed all the dragons who had been gathering nearby. Unlike the last time I had been in the council chambers, the doors were shut and the dragons outside wouldn't have been able to hear anything. They were clearly all curious, but none of us satisfied their curiosity.

Instead of giving them a show, we took the stairs in the tower down to the next floor and then the next until Brenta led us into a dining room of sorts.

Two big round tables formed a figure eight in the center of the room, and we headed to these as Griffin requested that food be brought up for all of us. The dragons who had been in the area took the rest of us in and seemed unsure what to make of us, but they didn't ask questions.

Drinks adorned a large side table, and plates, cutlery, and condiments were laid out on it. I assumed the food would be added once it was ready and appreciated the obvious station. It made deciding on the appropriate etiquette significantly easier.

No one spoke of anything important. The atmosphere was tense, and the conversation stayed on safer topics. Despite my declaration of not wanting the throne, an elder bowed at me as if I was his queen.

The food arriving a few minutes later was the perfect excuse for everyone to stop trying to engage in small talk for a moment and focus on eating instead. I appreciated the break—I felt as if I had aged a decade in a couple of days. To relax was a wonderful thing.

Before long, we were all having much more relaxed conversations and eating and drinking together as if we often did so. Ben and Jared were both good conversationalists and knew some of the council members well enough to ask about their personal lives and strike up interesting conversations.

I tried to join in as best I could, but this wasn't the area of life where I had much luck. Being socially awkward had been my MO for a long time, and being in my own social bubble in the city and out of it hadn't helped me make and keep friends.

By the time we'd finished eating and were ready to talk about more weighty subjects, the atmosphere had relaxed a little, and I was feeling ready to talk more about what I thought was best.

"I think we should discuss what we're going to tell the dragons of the city," I offered when no one seemed to want to begin a conversation.

"I don't think they need to know every last little detail,"

Brenta replied. "In fact, I'm not sure they need to know anything."

"They need to know that Scarlet volunteered to withdraw her claim to the throne. And that should paint Scarlet in a good light for doing so, and we should be united on it or our city won't heal," Griffin replied, but his voice was even more gentle than it had been earlier.

I appreciated it but didn't enter the conversation. It felt a little wrong to suggest what to say and try to control the narrative further. The dragons who didn't like me would need something they could believe coming from the elders they felt were on their side.

"Another thing we really need to consider is whether this is a permanent solution or a temporary one." The other female elder moved her chair a little closer. "It's worth looking at the laws. Scarlet, simply by being the heir, may need to be coronated anyway. She may decide to abdicate. But then it just means the throne passes to another red dragon. It doesn't necessarily mean we have no royal."

"Are there any other red dragons who aren't sitting in this room?" Ben asked.

No one knew the answer to that question, but the topic was interesting as they discussed the laws. It got more tense when Brenta again made it clear that she didn't want to follow the law if it meant putting anyone on a throne.

"I think we should put this aside for now," I said when it appeared as if Neritas was going to involve himself again and insist that if I was legally supposed to be crowned, I should be.

"This is an important matter. Unless you're saying that you'll abdicate if you do have to be crowned."

"Even then, it's an important matter. We should know if we need to find a relative," my mother put in. Although I still didn't know her well, I thought I was starting to get the idea of her emotions and body language, and I was pretty sure that she thought this funny in some way.

"Important or not, I want to make sure that we all get along and the evil is dealt with. I want the dragons of this world to continue to live both in harmony and safety. With the magic that I possess, I want to be able to help defend us. I can kill shadow catchers and I want to continue exploring the possibility that I can do more that would make this world safe."

The female elder smiled at me and gave me a nod.

"This is a noble goal, and if you not taking a crown can make this more of a reality, then I think that you should not take a crown. You clearly have a strong magical gift, and it gives me peace of mind to know that you have already made us safer by sending more evil to the underworld. Every time you do, you weaken our enemy and protect all of us."

It was the first time someone had made it clear that I was helping and that they wanted me to continue what I was doing. It was approval at a time I had not been getting much from outside my small friendship group.

"It's clear that we need to do more research and we need to figure out how we are going to talk about Scarlet's intentions. Why don't we all take a break, go away and research what we need to, and let Scarlet think about how she wishes to go about protecting us and what she believes that might look like. Her desire to do something other than rule may help us heal and unite the city, and our understanding of the law and our ability to effectively explain it can heal as well and possibly prevent further upset in the future if other information was learned." Griffin got up again as he spoke, giving Brenta several glances as he did.

Although it was a good conversation and I had been enjoying being in the room and being included, I got the impression I was now being asked to leave, along with my entourage, so they could talk more without me. I didn't feel entirely okay with what might happen once I did leave, but I was aware that I might not have much choice.

I got up and nodded respectfully toward everyone, but I didn't leave right away.

"Please also consider my mother as an elder. It might go a long way to healing the breach to see a red dragon be included, while it would not be me. And that's notwithstanding the teaching and understanding she has gained in many useful areas that could help her protect this city in another way."

"It is definitely something we will consider, assuming Sienna wishes to take on such a role?" Griffin turned to my mother.

"I would be honored. Although I had the misfortune not to get very much time with the late king, I was his confidante and I know that he both told me information and taught me many skills that were considered useful."

"Thank you. That is also very useful to know. The king was our protector for a long time and saw us through many hardships. Not all can remember his rule, but in general it was something considered good for us, I believe." Griffin smiled as my friends moved to the door and I waited for Mom to follow out with me.

Watching the reactions of the elders, I wasn't sure they all agreed with Griffin, but either way, it was time to go.

As I walked away, I realized how exhausted I was. The day had been a long one and I was not out of the woods. It seemed I had a lot to think about regarding my future.

CHAPTER FIVE

As the sun came up and the first rays shone around the blinds, I groaned. I had barely slept. After leaving the elders' private chambers, we had gone back to the royal apartments, and within a few minutes Griffin had arrived again and encouraged us to move to a different tower and different accommodations.

Still reeling, trying to process and aware that Neritas wasn't happy with me, I had packed everything I owned back up again and left my bedroom once more.

The guards had escorted us and our belongings several towers over to a large but not as plush family home. It was spread over several floors and only had one entrance. It was on the edge of the city and was therefore out of the way, but it also caught the predominant wind, which had been blowing in all night.

It was noisy and unfamiliar. The wind whistled past the walls of my bedroom. With everything I had been thinking over and my desires now open to me in a new way, I hadn't got much sleep.

Although Neritas and Flick had come from other homes, they were part of my family now. I quickly pulled some clothes on and left my room, and found them already in the dining room, drinking coffee and eating breakfast.

"You look as bad as we feel," Flick said.

"It's not easy getting used to this place." I sat and pulled a plate closer.

"I'm going to need earplugs if this is normal," Neritas added.

His bedroom was the other half of the same section of tower as mine and I didn't doubt that the wind had kept him up as much as it did me. None of us said much more until Ben appeared. He was also dressed and looked a little disheveled.

"Looks like you three are expected back in classes this morning. I've just been talking with Griffin and your mother."

I opened my mouth to tell him what I thought about the elders doing that without me present, but he was quicker than me.

"Your mother wanted to ask him some questions and I went with her. She wanted more information on the role of an elder and to make her request official in her own right. Griffin brought up what he thought would be a wise course of action for today."

"And he thinks I should just go back to classes?" I asked.

"Yes. Meanwhile, they will make a statement that you have currently opted to indefinitely postpone your coronation and will work with the elders to give more news shortly. That you want what is best for the city and that you want to give the dragons here time to express their concerns and desires for their future in more healthy ways."

I sighed, grateful that they had tried to word it well, but a little sad that it needed to be done at all. I knew that in some ways it would look as if I was giving in and running scared, but I also hoped it would counteract the fear people felt at the damage I had inflicted on other dragons with my shield.

The idea of going to classes after yesterday's events didn't make me any calmer or happier, but it would be best to get it over and done with. At some point I needed to leave the room.

"Do you think it's safe enough for Scarlet to go out there? I don't want us to get attacked again and her to get hurt or have to defend us, and then getting the blame for it." Neritas folded his arms.

"I think so. There aren't so many dragons keeping an eye on our tower, at least, and the general talk seems to be that Scarlet has done something that isn't expected of a red dragon and shows she has at least some kind of conscience. Some of the dragons in the city also understand what you are giving up," he said to me, "and that you went to a great deal of effort to heal the dragons who hurt you."

"That happened in the elders' chamber with the door shut," I replied, feeling shocked that anyone would know.

"They could have easily explained it to people," Ben added. "And you know how quickly gossip like new magic passes through the city."

It was a good point.

"Despite all that, I think there might be some merit to the three of you to train and make sure that you are able to defend yourselves. I'm not sure it will be needed, but who knows. This is uncharted territory for all of us."

Ben wasn't wrong, and the three of us needed something to do with our time anyway. We couldn't just mope around and hope that we would get what we wanted and stay safe.

I finished up my breakfast and got my sword and shield to begin training. Although Capricia had been able to give us some useful advice, it was a small relief to know that we didn't have to sneak out of the city and into danger to practice. The newer living arrangement gave us time and space to practice inside.

Flick was the last of us to be ready, but Ben and Mom also joined us, allowing me to draw on their magic a little. I made sure the shield and sword were charged, but not necessarily full. I didn't want to drain my family, just take enough to train.

If I'd thought Capricia had something to teach me about fighting, Mom ended up being even better. She was the only other person who had killed a shadow catcher that I knew of, and she had fought them many more times than I had. It wasn't a subject I brought up as I knew she bore several scars from fighting the demons.

She generally covered them up while in the city, although they hadn't been hidden when I met her. It gave me enough of an indication that they weren't something she wanted to talk about much.

"You already fight well," Mom said a few minutes later as I tried to imagine a shadow catcher in front of me and attack it.

The pride in her voice made me feel a lot better, but a

second later she corrected me and fixed other small mistakes in my technique and style. It was helpful but tiring, and it was hard to tell what she expected me to do differently sometimes.

I continued to fight and train for some time, and the focus kept my mind off other things threatening to stampede through it and bring me down. I hadn't wanted to be the queen, but stepping down because dragons who didn't know me were opposed to me becoming their ruler had hit me harder than I'd have admitted.

It was one thing to not want it and another entirely to be despised by so many others.

By the end of the first hour, I was so exhausted that I called a halt to the training. Neritas and Flick were both drenched in sweat and panting, and they fell back onto a sofa as soon as they could stop defending against my attacks or attacking me as if they were shadow catchers.

My arms ached, but it was the gentle burn of muscles that weren't used to being used so much and was a strange, comforting feeling that seemed right for the level of effort I had put in. Mom exhaled as I stopped pulling on the magic from her, Ben, even though he wasn't with us, and my two friends. They were happy to lend me theirs, especially when it powered a device they found useful, but it didn't stop me feeling guilty when I did it and saw the impact it had on them.

"Do you think we'll run into more of them?" Flick asked a moment later.

"If we leave the city, there's a good chance. Whether I rule or not, I'm still the only red dragon who can charge the gate, and they seem to know that. Even without Fintar,

I might have to face them." I sighed and threw myself down on the sofa in between my two friends.

"You will definitely have to face them again." My mom looked off into the distance as she spoke, almost as if she was remembering something.

I didn't interrupt, letting the silence hang in case she thought of something we ought to know. She was our sole source of genuine information about my family line now.

"Fintar may be gone, and it might mean a sort of reprieve, but it won't last. Just like your father and I, and probably every red dragon since the beginning of time, the shadow catchers will treat us as if we're a very different species."

This was something I feared. While I was capable of fighting them and had killed plenty, at some point my luck would run out. Eventually, one of them would catch me at the wrong moment and end my life. It was inevitable. Fight enough battles, and no matter how good you are, you'll eventually lose to someone.

At least, that was the logic that made me wary to hunt the creatures and keep engaging them. While I wanted to protect the world, I had to pick my battles. And that was what I was doing right now.

Ben came through a short while later and smiled, looking over the exhausted forms of everyone around me and the sword and shield I was holding again.

"Looks like you've decided to keep training the skill that got you in trouble," he remarked as he sat on the front sofa by the window.

"As much as possible without being stupid about it. I've got to do something."

"It was very bold of you to do what you did in the elders' chambers yesterday." Ben didn't take his eyes off me as he spoke. "I know that can't have been easy for you, and I have no idea if it was the right choice, but I do know that you have a wonderful heart and your sacrifice and willingness to do what's in your power to protect dragons and their right to decide is honorable."

I swallowed the lump in my throat, not sure how to respond to the vote of confidence.

Neritas put his arm around me and gave me a sideways hug for a moment.

"We're all proud of you and you've got our support. If you want to leave this place and go somewhere where they will be more rational and not too stupid to live, then I'll come with you."

"Like, another city?" I asked Neritas. I was never sure how I felt when his hugs lingered, though he never appeared to expect anything more.

"Another city, not a city of dragons. Whatever. You've got the support from Cios and Jace. You've got Alitas too, right?"

I nodded. He was listing some powerful dragons. But even with all of them together, we'd be short of enough dragons to stay safe or make a more rigorous claim to a throne. And I still needed to figure out how to power the gate.

"While it's tempting to run away, this city is where most of my ancestors used to live. I am hoping that the rest of the information I need to keep that gate closed can be found here somewhere. That the elders will trot out something or someone that gives them proof and a reason to work with me. And in the meantime, I still have stuff to learn and more to look for in that vault. I might not be the queen, but it was my father's. I could make a claim to it."

Neritas grinned and got to his feet. "That sounds like something I can help with. Go check out the vault where I found those two things and see if anything else feels like it might be similar."

"I also know where I can be useful," Ben added. "I will continue translating and investigating books and studies on anything that might further our cause. My access to the library is almost unparalleled."

Mom smiled and gave me a large hug. "And I will do what I do best and help train you to fight while also making myself valuable in the community as a healer. I know there's less I can do to help, but after all these years of waiting and hoping to be able to even get a glimpse of you, I'm just grateful to be involved in your world again."

With everyone having pledged themselves to a task and already getting on with them, it just left Flick. He looked at me and shrugged.

"My best skill is flying, and at the moment you're so much better than you were that there's nothing I can teach you or suggest you do better. I can be a pretty face and let you use the magic and skills I possess as they become more relevant."

"You're never just a pretty face," I replied without missing a beat. "And you have many uses. While we're figuring all this out, I could also do with getting an idea of how everyone is reacting to everything that has happened. Everyone likes you, even with you being my friend and protecting me."

Flick got up and smiled at me with a gratitude that made him light up.

"Just when I think that you can't get better as a person, you show that you have a brain and know us all well. I will take my task seriously and gather what I can by way of opinions. And if I can, I will encourage positivity."

"Be careful," I said, amused by his enthusiasm. "Some of them could decide to be aggressive and not kind."

Flick nodded but gave me a grin anyway before spinning around and making his way out of the apartment. I watched him go and felt nervous for him. Although it seemed like a frivolous task, it wasn't.

None of us had it easy, but Flick was probably the most vulnerable of us, and I fought the urge to fetch him back and ask him to do something else. He had been pleased with the task I gave him and knew it was something he would be good at. I hoped that no one harmed him.

CHAPTER SIX

My stomach was full of butterflies as I moved to the entrance of the apartment. I was tired, but glad it was a new day. After everything that had happened the day before, I was worried about my lessons and how they would go. The city knew I had withdrawn my claim to the throne and planned to leave the throne empty for now.

Despite that, I had insisted that my genealogy be officially changed and my mom and real father now attached to me. The elders had agreed to it. The presence of a mother who was certain of my father's identity was considered enough proof by the records office, and that had been fed to them. Given that I wasn't asking for preferential treatment, they had agreed at least for my records to show whom I belonged to.

There were a lot of dragons flying around the towers nearby, many of them circling and looking for me, no doubt. I knew these dragons could be hostile and that, for some reason, Capricia had decided that she didn't like me or want to protect me.

After Flick had returned the previous evening, he had gone through a lot of what he'd overheard. He admitted that it had been hard for him to get anyone to talk to him at first, but some alcohol in the right person had eventually got a few dragons to talk more. It was a strange way of gathering information, but it worked.

The city wasn't as angry as it had seemed to us at first. The dragons were confused and not sure what they wanted, and while they appreciated that I was powerful, they didn't think the dragon race needed a queen. Flick had told them that the gate needed to be charged and that the same ability I'd used with the shield could be used to do it.

He had no idea if the word would spread, but he'd planted the idea and it was unlikely to be traced back to him. It also had a chance of not being believed, however, or dismissed as a fanciful conspiracy theory.

I'd hoped to find out exactly what had made Capricia decide not only that she disliked me but that I didn't count as a citizen of her city who deserved her protection. Especially after we had fought shadow catchers and a handler side by side, something about her demeanor had struck me as strange.

Flick hadn't learned anything about the guards and their attitude or what the elders were likely to do, but he'd gotten some info from the other citizens that helped calm me and made me worry at the same time. If they were confused, they could be easily led by someone vocal. I was grateful they weren't all ready to hate me yet.

There had been a lot of curiosity about how I had defended myself, and Flick had observed the two dragons who had been hurt by my defense telling everyone what had happened. They hadn't been as kind as I hoped, but the proof was staring people in the face. Both dragons were walking and talking, better healed than they might have otherwise been.

Flick came out of his room and over to me, ready to go. Neritas was already with me, and Ben had come up with some reasons to go with me as far as the library as well. It was sweet of him.

My mom looked as if she also wanted to join me, but I said goodbye. It was better for her to be in the rooms and safe than for me to also be worrying about her well-being. We didn't have many lessons that day, and those that I did have were usually friendly enough, with teachers that treated me with respect.

"Ready?" Neritas asked when I still didn't move.

Truthfully, I was terrified, but I was going to have to go anyway and do my best to make the most of it. I couldn't hide in the tower forever. I needed to try to live a normal life.

We'd all agreed to walk the entire way, knowing that being in human form would make us appear to be a little less threatening, if nothing else.

There had been a big debate on whether I should carry the shield and sword. They were clearly weapons and might make it seem as if I was expecting to have to use them again to defend myself. Now everyone knew that they could hurt others in combat, no one would want to see them on me, especially when I should just be going to lessons.

With that in mind, I had agreed to leave them behind in

the apartment. I'd been carrying them around for so many days in a row now that I felt strange without them, and part of me wanted to take them anyway, driven by an unease in my body.

"I've got my city shield," Neritas pointed out when he caught me looking in that direction. "If you really needed it, you could take this, and I'd fly over to get yours within a minute or two."

Although he was trying to reassure me, I also knew that the scenario of that fateful day wouldn't have given him the chance to fly off and get what I needed. There were too many attackers and they had pinned us to one space.

Of course, they were aiming for me more than anyone else, so if I had moved away from Neritas, he might have had the opportunity to get me more help. It wasn't a scenario I'd planned for, and I didn't want to think about it now, but I had to consider it.

"You've done what the city needs, and everyone told me that you had helped by letting go of the throne," Flick added. "It's going to be a little bit more awkward than normal, but give it time and it will calm again."

I exhaled. Flick was probably right, and either way, it was time to go.

We moved as a group and crossed a bridge to another tower before winding down. I didn't have any flying lessons today and wouldn't have gone to them if I had. All we had was a history lesson and a science lesson about some of the tech that the dragon community used.

At the beginning, I had found the lessons hit-and-miss in terms of enjoyment and usefulness. Having not grown up in the city, they were lessons that helped explain the culture and place I was trying to fit into, but they also could be boring and difficult depending on what they were trying to explain. The history was clearly modified and left out some of the most important elements for some reason. And the tech class sometimes went over tech from the human world that I had been using for my entire life.

That made the lessons the perfect ones to attend—easy and not overstimulating the brain would be good for keeping the emotions in check.

I wasn't able to be entirely calm today, however. I just couldn't be.

The first lesson was a significant distance from the apartment, and as we traveled through the city I noticed that everyone who came across us stared, and the atmosphere grew icy and cold. Even the guards that lingered here and there, meant to help be a symbol of safety, were cold and avoided making eye contact with me.

I tried to smile at dragons I recognized, especially if they had been warm in the past, but no one acknowledged me or returned my greetings. None of it helped my fear, and before long, my heart was racing and I was struggling to have a positive attitude or smile at anyone.

Neritas and Flick stuck with me. Neritas, at least, was more used to getting a frosty reception wherever he went. I didn't relax when I reached the class either, although I saw Neritas let out a deep breath and Flick smile and return to his jovial self.

The atmosphere in this room was tense as well, but the best I could do was try to ignore it and focus on the lesson. It was easier said than done, but the class was soon as full as usual, and the teacher came in. He also ignored me, not meeting my gaze and acting as if I wasn't there.

For now, being ignored was better than the alternatives. I would take it. It would allow me to get through the day and get back to the apartment. I could only hope that time made me an accepted, or at least tolerated, member of the society again.

The minutes ticked slowly by as we learned about some minor conflict between dragons when the countries they were in went to war, and how some took sides and risked exposure to change the course of history. I was bored, but also grateful that it was a lesson I didn't have to think too hard for. I simply had to absorb information and let everyone get used to me being among them again.

The teacher continued to ignore me, not asking me to answer any questions and not calling on me to read anything. I was grateful for it.

Eventually it came to an end, and the teacher swiftly excused himself and left the room. Immediately the tension came back, and my fellow dragons glanced at me and each other. It was as if they were all waiting for someone to be a ringleader and ask a question, but I got the feeling it wasn't a question I wanted to answer.

I got up and felt Flick and Neritas fall in beside me immediately. A single look their way showed me that they were also tense and picking up on the vibe of the room. We weren't yet at the classroom door when the dragons around us formed up and blocked our way, most of them folding their arms.

Looking around at them, my heart started to race. This

wasn't good. If I didn't diffuse this somehow, I got the feeling that everything was going to go horribly wrong.

"I know you're all angry at me and don't like me, but I just want to go to my lessons and try to live like a normal dragon in the city. I don't want to hurt anyone, fight anyone, or do anything but keep the shadow catchers away from all of us and keep this world safe."

"Bitch, please. We all know that you want to be our queen and have us all bow at your feet. You think that you're better than us, just like every other red dragon."

I shook my head, but I didn't see the point in arguing about it. If they didn't believe me and had made up their minds, trying to refute them wasn't going to help either.

"It's common knowledge that you don't like red dragons, but Scarlet is more concerned with keeping us safe than taking a throne. That's why she's let go of her claim. But we will defend her if you guys get aggressive, and you know that both us and her can do a lot of damage." Flick crossed his arms in an uncharacteristically macho display.

This seemed to delay the anger, but only for a moment.

"You've drunk the Kool-Aid and you've gone and supported an insane dragon who thinks she's far more important than she is."

"I don't think I'm important. At least not more than any of you. I wanted none of this. The human world was a place I was happy in, but the shadow catchers won't leave me alone."

"Well, we don't want you either. Go back to your humans and see if they'll worship at your feet." The female dragon in front of me who'd said this narrowed her eyes and stepped closer as she spoke. Almost immediately, she became the ringleader. Several of them echoed her words, throwing them at me again and again.

I exhaled as I tried to think of something else to do or say. There was no getting through to them, but despite their words, they all stood in the way.

"If you want Scarlet gone, then it would make sense to let us through so we can take her from your presence. I'm sure we can go back to our rooms and give you all some time for—"

"No. We want her gone, but not until she's answered for everything she's done. Not until she knows her place again."

A shudder rippled through me as the male dragon who spoke the words stepped forward, his hands bunching into fists. Flick and Neritas came in closer, and I heard the crackle of electricity as Flick made it move across his knuckles. A warning that he would defend me. I raised my hands in a surrender pose.

"Come on. You don't want to start a fight. Whether I win or get put back in my place, or any number of other outcomes, a bunch of dragons will get hurt and I don't want that for sure. I only want to use my abilities to fight demons, as we all should."

"You just can't stop thinking you're better than us, can you?" the same guy asked right before he lunged for me.

So many dragons surged forward, all of the ones to the sides and behind attacking, that Neritas and Flick were overwhelmed. I was grabbed by so many hands and pulled about that I could do nothing to defend myself.

I panicked and drew on the magic around them, then hardened and charged the clothes around me with the black dragon magical ability. It protected most of my body as the first few punches hit me.

Pain flared everywhere that I couldn't easily protect. My arms and head were exposed, and I tried to cover my face, feeling jostled and pulled about, struggling to focus on the magic as more and more of me hurt.

At some point I went down, knocked or shoved over, desperately trying to think of some magic I could do that would defend me and not hurt them. I curled up, bringing my arms up around my head as I did my best to protect my face.

Although I felt the connection to Neritas and Flick and they were practically pushing their magic onto me to use, I didn't know exactly where they were. I wanted to tell them to run, but I also wanted to have someone come to my rescue. I'd never been so scared or hurt so much, and it didn't let up.

It took several more seconds for me to register that I was making a strange keening sound and whimpering every time another foot or hand connected with me. Sometimes it didn't hurt—my mind managed to keep my clothes hardened and protecting my body, but if it caught my skin, it flared more pain until I was sure bones were broken and I was feeling fuzzy headed.

I shifted, trying to get away, but the blows came from all sides. I had lost my two companions somewhere, and all I could think from then was how much I hoped the same wasn't happening to them. Neither of them would have been able to protect themselves.

CHAPTER SEVEN

Yelling sounded from somewhere nearby, but it only added to the commotion until I felt the connection of more dragons, familiar dragons who came rushing closer to me. I reached for their magic, knowing they wouldn't mind as much, grateful for the fresh black dragons among them.

As suddenly as the assault began, it stopped.

I didn't move at first. The pain was so intense and my relief so complete when the attack stopped that I lay still and hoped it wouldn't start again. My eyes were tightly shut, but I felt dragons moving around me and didn't want to do anything that would encourage anyone to start hurting me again.

"Clear out. The bullying and abuse are not happening here any longer. All of you should be ashamed of yourselves. Dragons are on earth to protect, not to beat the crap out of someone who isn't defending themselves." Ben's voice came through strong and clear, but I had no idea if it would have any impact on them.

It cut through the pain a little, but not enough to make

me want to move or do anything but continue to whimper and hold as still as I could so it wouldn't hurt more than necessary. The room quieted and I felt a hand reach out to my side.

"Scarlet." Neritas' gentle voice came from just in front of me.

I didn't respond. It hurt to move, and I didn't want to try.

"Can you move at all? Is anything numb, or does it hurt?" Neritas didn't give up, his hand stroking gently down my side and back up again.

"I hurt everywhere I didn't harden my clothes into a shield." I took my time and moved slowly, as if to confirm my words. My cheeks were wet with tears beneath my arms and felt cold as I uncurled a little.

A pained groan escaped me as Neritas tried to scoop me up into his arms.

"Careful. Her spine could have taken damage."

I slowly shook my head to reassure them as I felt Neritas pause with me part way into his arms and held in an awkward position. More hands reached for me, careful to touch only where I was covered with clothing as much as possible. It wasn't long before I was cradled up against Neritas, my head resting on his shoulder and his arms around me.

Ben gingerly wrapped a cloak around me and over all the parts of me already sporting bruises, and Flick wiped the tears off my face with a tissue as gently as he could. Tiffany also came close and neatened my hair a little.

Although I appreciated the concern, I just wanted to be anywhere else than here. I saw several teachers in the background, along with guards from around the city. All of them were in human form, with concern on their faces, and it made me feel worse. I wanted to hide and run away from the entire city.

"I'm going to take you back to the apartment," Neritas said quietly enough that only I would hear. "Can you cope with that?"

"Yes," I whispered back, grateful that my mouth was already close enough to his ear so I didn't have to move or speak up.

I slowly moved one arm under the cloak to hold on to the opposite shoulder. It had the added benefit of shielding my face from more angles. Ben, Flick, the guards, and all the teachers fell in around. As soon as we were outside, two of the guards took dragon form and circled us as Neritas took the bridges and stairs toward the right tower.

Pain flared with every step, especially when Neritas had to go upward, but I was more concerned about the weight Neritas was carrying and how difficult this must be for him to carry me so far. I wasn't the lightest person in the world, and he had a long way up to go.

Still, he didn't complain, and he got me there. My mother rushed over to me as soon as we walked through the door. The fear on her face deepened when she saw me.

"What happened?" she demanded. The imperious tone in her voice reminded me that she had once been the partner of a king.

Flick filled her in as Neritas carried me to the sofa and gently sat me down. I couldn't help but whimper as the pain flared again. He tried to move as slowly as possible, but I caught the look of exhaustion in his eyes. He was barely holding it together.

As soon as I was set down and he'd extracted his arms, he covered me with the cloak more evenly and sat on the floor beside me.

"Thank you." I looked him in the eye. It hurt, but I wanted him to know how grateful I was that he hadn't left me and had pushed himself so far beyond his limits to get me to the tower. I drew a small amount of magic from the dragons in the room, combined it, and gently fed it to Neritas and Flick.

Their eyes went wide, and Neritas rested a hand over my arm to stroke it gently through the cloak. It was sweet of him, but the moment passed when my mother and Ben came over to me, now filled in on what had happened.

"Inform the elders," Ben said to Flick. "They need to know what goes on in the city and they won't get this version of events from anyone else in a hurry."

I tried to consider what this would mean for my future here, but I was in too much pain to think clearly. I just wanted to retreat into my head and let my thoughts drift or focus on something that would take the pain away.

Before long, Mom was at my side with the healing device in her hands. All the other dragons in the room came closer, every dragon color represented between the teachers, guards, and my family and friends. They were the fuel as Mom pulled the cloak away to heal some of the damage done.

Her first target was my left arm. The bone was obviously broken in several places. Ben helped her set it while I looked away and Neritas helped me hold still, my head buried in his shoulder again briefly. I whimpered into him, grateful it stifled the noise before the healing device started to work and heal the break.

Slowly the pain faded, but it didn't go away entirely, settling into a dull ache. I breathed more easily as Mom moved on to other difficult areas. I was covered in bruises, many of them already beginning to darken and purple all over my skin, especially my arms, but they soon grew better as well.

By the time she was done, Griffin was standing nearby, silently surveying all the damage being healed and the situation I was in. I still hurt when she stopped, and my body felt weak.

I tilted my head back for a moment and closed my eyes to focus my mind. This was the worst pain I'd ever been in, and I wanted to just sleep and demand painkillers. Even after the help from the healing device, I was struggling to cope. I didn't want to be grilled by the elders.

Griffin crouched by my side.

"I've heard enough to know this isn't what the city I have served ought to be like or to have done. You have my sincere apologies for what has happened."

"It's not your fault. They were bullies and I was an easy target. I think it's best I don't go to lessons for a while."

"I agree. Rest for a while and I will bring the elders to you. I believe we need to have another session and discuss how we move forward. It is our duty to protect you and we need to find an appropriate response to the behavior of these dragons."

Although I wanted to add more of my thoughts on that, I didn't have the focus to get my mind together.

Right now, I wanted nothing more than to rest. I shifted just enough to get comfortable and closed my eyes. For now, I didn't want to know what was going to happen or why.

I came to several hours later, the sun setting on the far side of the tower. Neritas was still sitting near the sofa on the floor, his head tilted back against my leg. He was asleep, but my sword and shield were resting between us on the floor.

As soon as I opened my eyes, Mom and Ben came over. Ben placed a tray of food gently on my lap while Mom ran the healing device over me again.

The tray also held some painkillers and a large drink of water beside the amazing-smelling stew. I didn't want to move, still hurting and covered in bruises, but I wasn't going to sit around like I was sick and needed caring for either. I was a red dragon, and even if I wasn't claiming the throne, I was the rightful heir.

After my rest, a fire and determination had come back to me. I didn't know how long I had been out, but with my mother helping to take away more pain and the sword and shield nearby reminding me that I had been tested by my ancestors and found worthy, I was more determined than ever to find a way to unite all dragons, whether I wore my crown or not.

I took the pills and ate, the extra healing boost taking a little more of the pain away and the painkillers taking enough of the rest that I could function without wincing every five seconds and wishing I could fall back into the oblivion of deep sleep.

By the time I had finished eating, Mom was also done, and the elders had been notified that I was awake. Neritas still didn't leave his position near me, and Flick wasn't far away either. It looked as if he hadn't left my side the entire time. They were good friends, but not for the first time I wondered if they were hoping to be more than friends to me.

When I had found out who I was and learned of the dragon world's objection to my mother and her coloring not being pure, it had made me wonder about Neritas and Flick and how protective they were of me. Did they know that I couldn't consider a future with either of them? Not unless there were no red dragons left and nothing else could be done to have a completely pure red dragon line.

I had no way of knowing what they were thinking, and I wasn't going to ask. Not now and not here. Not when I could offer them nothing but a mess and a failed claim to a throne. Neritas had wanted me to be so much more. It made it hard to look at him sometimes, to know I had disappointed him.

Before I could do more than get up off the sofa, wincing a couple of times as Neritas helped me turn and clip my sword and shield to the belt on my waist, the elders appeared. They each flew in through the open door, transforming as they did and doing so with elegance that reminded me of how much I used to struggle with my own transformations.

Within a minute they all stood in the room as well, Capricia and several guards with them.

"We need to talk." I knew this would be far more awkward outside of the elders' chambers, but I was unsure that I could get my hurt body all the way to their tower either way.

"That's why we're all here. You look as if you're doing better than Griffin suggested your injuries would allow." Brenta looked me over with no compassion. She sounded almost as if she thought they had wasted their time.

"My mother helped heal me faster than normal, the same way I demonstrated before you all the other day, and I am determined to do what I need to despite all the obstacles put in my way." I met her gaze with a fierceness that made her blink and eyes widen for a moment.

"Then we're grateful once more for the abilities your kind possesses," Griffin replied. He motioned for the rest of the elders to head to the dining table as if they owned the place, but I didn't let this get to me. For now, they were above me in rank and I would have to accommodate them.

I followed along with my mother, Ben, Neritas, Flick, Reijo, and Capricia. It was a strange gathering. Some of them were firm allies of mine, and waves of animosity came off others, but I tried to ignore the latter and focus on what was needed.

"Once again, you have my sincere apologies that you were attacked not once but twice while in the city." Griffin started the meeting in a kinder tone, but it wasn't a sentiment all the dragons shared. Brenta looked away as he spoke, and Capricia folded her arms across her chest as if she didn't care.

"Thank you. I think it's become clear that I can't stay in Detaris. I'm never going to be entirely welcome here, and having attempted to claim the throne, there are too many dragons who are going to hold that against me. I need to give them time to cool off, if not to mature." I met Capricia's gaze as I spoke this last word, emphasizing it.

"You can't leave," Flick said, shaking his head. "This city needs you. It might not realize it, but you have already done so much to protect us. Fought and killed so many shadow catchers."

"Something we only have your word for," Brenta replied without missing a beat.

"Have not several of us attested to that? And in the elders' chambers where you can tell if we're lying?" The pain was making me too grouchy to beat around the bush or be polite this time. I was done with their crap.

I unfixed the shield from my waist, putting it down on the table. At the same time, I charged it, lighting up the lines across it until it made the room glow.

"I'm leaving. But I still want what I've always wanted. I intend to protect this city and all the other dragons on this planet. I'll go somewhere I am wanted and work out how to stop the gate weakening from there. If you crown me or not, when the time comes, I will call on all of you and I will expect you to encourage the dragons you care for and are responsible for to help charge the gate."

Griffin nodded without hesitation.

"That's assuming the gate is weakening. We don't know that for sure." Capricia came away from the wall and up to the table beside Brenta. I saw the elder smirk for the briefest of seconds before returning to the impassive look she'd held before.

Feeling the venomousness in them, I hesitated. It

seemed I was going to have to fight the elders and the majority of the city every step of the way, but I had to find something that would unite them, whether they liked me or not.

Somehow.

CHAPTER EIGHT

The silence in the room grew more awkward as I tried to think of something that would break the tension.

"The gate has held all our lives," a female elder said. Her face showed concern, and I felt a wave of gratitude toward her. "What makes you think it's weakening now? I know you've claimed it before, and you clearly believe it yourself enough that our chamber finds no lie in your faith that it's true. But what is that belief based upon?"

"Seeing it with my own eyes and hearing from those who guard it more closely." I didn't hesitate to respond, but it seemed to make no difference. Capricia scoffed.

"You heard it from Jace and the terrorist cell she now serves. Not exactly dragons we trust or who have acted honorably. They could be spinning this to try and control you. To get you to make the world safer out there by fighting shadow catchers when you don't need to. Or by drawing their attention here when—"

"I haven't killed any shadow catchers that weren't already coming after me for some reason," I cut Capricia off, wondering where all this was coming from when she had been with me and seen so much with her own eyes. She'd stood beside me in battle and fought the shadow catchers when they kept coming for me.

I didn't say anything else, not wanting to antagonize things further, but I was prepared to have to fight for the idea that the gate might need help. They so badly wanted to think everything was okay that they were willing to pretend nothing was wrong despite the evidence I had already presented. It didn't bode well.

"We've all heard you say this before and known the truth of your words. Capricia herself has also presented to us her appreciation of what happened the last time you left the city and corroborated much of your story, although it's clear that time has changed everyone's perception of what all these events mean, as time is wont to do." Griffin frowned as he paused, his voice seeming to break through the tension, much to my gratitude.

"I think time has given Capricia a better sense of reality," Brenta slotted in the gap.

"That may be true and it might not. Only time can prove if our actions and words are the right viewpoint or not. I think this is a matter that I will need to see for myself, however," Griffin replied.

These words were met with a stunned silence.

"You can't mean leaving the city to go to the gate," a female asked. Griffin nodded.

"You'll get yourself killed, or worse, bring even more attention to our kind. It's bad enough that there's a social media video circulating of Scarlet and her...companions fighting shadow catchers in broad daylight outside a restaurant." Brenta looked as if she'd happily have murdered me for the latter if she thought that she could get away with it.

"I would be in some danger, yes, of this I am sure. But I have been an elder of this city for only a couple of months less than you, Brenta, and my viewpoint, experience, and understanding have all been appreciated in the past. If I sought out the truth of this matter and brought my own personal findings back to the city, we could all act with more understanding of what we might or might not be facing."

Some of the other elders nodded as if this was a viewpoint they had considered but weren't sure how to articulate. Brenta and Capricia didn't look happy with this, Capricia especially.

"You can't go alone," Ben pointed out, and I had a pretty good inkling of what would follow this.

"I'm sure that the two people who can protect me best will understand the importance and my need for their aid and accompaniment," Griffin said. "Scarlet, Capricia, you are clearly capable of fighting off the vile shadow catchers between you. Yet you also represent the two opposing viewpoints presented to the elders better than anyone else here. I would humbly request that you come with me and help protect me so I can make a full report to the elders on the matters upon my return."

I nodded and tried to wash away how slimy I felt agreeing to partner with Capricia when I had already provided the proof that the elders sought. This was unnecessary in so many ways. It did give me another path forward and another chance and potential ally in my quest, however.

Capricia took a little longer to give her assent, but eventually she also nodded. Looking as if he'd been invited to a garden party with the queen, Griffin jumped up and smiled.

"It's settled then. We shall go to the gate and you two will protect me. I will present my findings to the elders as soon we're back."

Another elder chimed in, "While I think this is highly irregular, I must confess to not being sure what is going on. Having one of us who has seen everything perfectly clearly will be a huge boon and help my consideration process considerably."

This was enough that it seemed to finally settle the entire matter. I wasn't going to stay in the city, but for reasons I hadn't anticipated. The elders decided this concluded the matter on the agenda, and it made anger flare in me again. Not one of them had assured me that they would do anything about the violence I had been subjected to. It was clear that they didn't care for me right now.

"I guess I'd best pack up again, but I'm bringing extra shields this time." Capricia almost growled the words as she stalked off after the elders. None of my companions spoke as she left. All of them had witnessed the entire thing without saying much or giving their emotions away, but that courtesy to the elders vanished as soon as it was only me and them left.

"What a bunch of bullshit," Neritas declared. "They

want you to use skills that keep them safe and turn you into nothing but a glorified nursemaid."

"That they may do, but Griffin is one of the few elders I have any faith of putting what we provide him to good use instead of trying to undermine everything to retain power." I tried to speak as evenly as I could.

I couldn't know what their real motivation was, so I simply checked that I had everything I needed in my pack and nothing important would be left behind.

"You know that we're all coming with you, right?" Neritas came to my side again. "There's no way we're letting you walk into danger without us there to help protect you and lend you our magic."

"But it puts all of you in danger as well."

"Need we remind you that we've just faced a whole bunch of angry dragons by your side here?" Flick grinned as he stood beside Neritas. "You're a red dragon. It would appear that you're in danger wherever you go. Besides, I've always wanted to be part of the honor guard. They have the best fliers, best magic users, and the most loyal dragons on the planet. That's why they're called honor guards."

"I'd have to officially be royalty to have honor guards," I pointed out.

"The only reason you're not already crowned our queen is because a bunch of dragons in this city would rather pretend everything is just fine and they don't need anyone else. We all know that you're the queen anyway. Just because some won't recognize you, it doesn't stop you being the heir. It doesn't stop you being the only dragon with the power to save us all and it doesn't take away the honor of protecting you and helping you in your calling."

"Hear, hear," Ben agreed as he and Reijo fell in on either side.

I shook my head and exhaled, mystified yet grateful that they believed I was worth so much. I still didn't want the pressure or the role, but they were right about one thing: no one else could save us all, and I believed we needed saving. Whether I wanted to or not, I had to try. And I needed their help to do it.

"Okay, get packed up and ready to head out as soon as everyone else is. I'll contact Jace and get her to meet us with a team to take us to the gate." It was the only concession I could make, but it broadened the grins on all their faces. They rushed away to do exactly that, leaving me with my mother.

She came over to me and took my hands in hers, moving slowly to not hurt me more than necessary.

"I know this isn't easy and I wouldn't wish the role you play on anyone, but for what it's worth, I'm proud of you. If anyone can find a way to unite the dragons and bring them together, you can."

"I'm not sure I can. A bunch of them just willingly beat the crap out of me because they hate me so much."

"They don't hate you. They hate what they think you represent. They want more freedom than they have. To feel as if their lives mean something and that they're also important. You have to get them to see everything differently. You've inspired so many to already willingly give their lives to this cause. You can turn this around. I know you can."

Searching my mother's eyes, I looked for any doubt in

them, but she looked at me with love, pride, and support. It helped.

"Okay, I might need some help packing," I admitted a few seconds later, the pain still a lot to handle.

Mom nodded and helped me get back to my room to figure out what to take with me. Before I began, I messaged Jace, filling her in briefly on the need to show the elders the gate to convince them I was speaking the truth and asking her assistance in escorting them there safely.

I was partway through gathering all the clothes I needed and deciding what basics I wanted on top when I got a reply.

> You're in luck, Red. I'm in the area and got a team with me. Not surprised those crusty old dragons are trying to deny the need to actually make some important decisions. I'd love to show them the seriousness of the situation and see if we can whip some life into their old bones yet. Let me know where you need me and when and I'll be there.

I grinned at the bluntness of the words. She'd always seemed to get me, and she had this healthy disrespect for authority and a willingness to speak her mind that I appreciated. At the same time, she wanted to get the job done and do what was needed. I could see why she also didn't feel as if she could fit into the city.

I replied with a time estimate and a rough direction and distance from the city, and asked her to wait for us to find her. I doubted it would help my cause if the dragons who didn't trust me saw me interacting with dragons they thought were terrorists. In my experience, however, the city was full of toxic behavior and the dragons outside were those who had broken free.

Once my clothes were tucked into my rucksack along with some basic accessories and snacks and I had my sword and shield properly strapped to my waist again, I considered the small box of precious items I now had. The crown my father had worn as a dragon was in there, along with everything else of significance to me—the journals Anthony had left me and a few other small trinkets and possessions I had from before I'd known I was a red dragon.

Although I had left most of these here the other times I'd left the city, something about leaving this time made me want to take them all with me. I might not come back, even if I returned the elder. Given how hostile everyone had been, the part of me that tried to be prepared for all possibilities told me to take them all with me and keep them safe under my protection.

I voiced the concern to my mother. She looked at me for a moment, and I half expected her to tell me not to be so silly.

"If your gut is telling you to keep them safe somewhere else, listen to your gut. At worst, they'll come with us and come back again with no trouble."

Once again, my mother said the words I needed to hear. It made me feel a lot better about taking the smaller things and the journal and tucking them into my rucksack among everything else. I removed a sweatshirt to fit the crown in as well, and tucked my clothes around it to pack it safely so it wouldn't break.

It was a good thing I only expected to be away from the city for a couple of days, given how full the rucksack was. By the time it was done, I was hurting badly again, my arms especially.

Although I had taken my time to pack and fussed over taking everything precious with me, I was the first from my group to be ready to leave. It gave Mom time to help me heal again. Using the device so often was taking its toll on her, so I tried to take over and use it myself, but she stopped me.

"We are going somewhere dangerous where all the fight will be coming toward you. You need to be as strong as possible. Let me do this and then rest. I'll be fine."

"Don't do too much then." I didn't like everyone making so many sacrifices for me.

"Even if I wanted to, I couldn't. This thing can only do so much in a certain time frame. If you weren't in so much pain, I wouldn't be trying to use it again so soon."

I opened my mouth to tell her I wasn't in too much pain, but she raised her eyebrow in anticipation of my denial, and I knew that she wouldn't hear it. In truth, I still hurt a lot. The mass of dragons willing to hurt me had done a lot of damage. So much so that, had we not had magic to heal me, I was sure I wouldn't be able to function and feared I might even have died. I'd bled internally a lot, according to my mother.

Even with the healing, I felt weaker than I ever had, but I was trying to hide that too. I had to keep going and be strong for the sake of all the dragons around me.

CHAPTER NINE

By the time about half of the group was ready, Griffin had returned with a packed bag and a smile on his face. He looked genuinely excited to be leaving the city and going to see the gate for himself, and once again I was struck by how difficult it must be for most of them to live in one city and never leave it.

"Before we leave, I have been asked by the other elders to remind you that we need to fly beneath the radar—pardon the pun—for this task. They are very anxious that there won't be any more social media videos of us fighting demons, and they're aware that there has been some news of our kind or abilities every time you have left the city." Although he said the words gently and looked at me with warmth, I caught a tone of exasperation behind the words. I had no idea if it was directed at me.

"I will do my best, but I can make no promises, when in every single one of those instances I was attacked. But I would also caution you on this matter. There is a good chance that we will be fighting shadow catchers at some point."

"This is something I have already considered. I remain optimistic, as Capricia does, that you and her working to dispatch this handler who had been guiding them all will have made things considerably safer."

"I share the hope, but less of the optimism." It was all I could say to warn him, and I wasn't going to waste my breath. Time would prove one of us right, and I genuinely hoped it was him. I let him bask in his positive feeling for now.

Neritas appeared back next, a familiar shield also at his waist. It was the one I'd taken from the fallen enemy in our last battle, and it was similar to the one he'd found me in the vaults of the city. If the elders realized that was where I had got mine, they hadn't said anything, and no one had tried to take his either.

I instinctively reached out to everyone to pull the power to charge it before I realized what I'd done.

"Well, that was a new feeling," Griffin said.

Feeling like a deer in headlights, I didn't reply, not sure how to explain what I'd done and feeling instantly guilty for taking his magic without permission. Doing it in an emergency and for defense was something I felt much better about, but this had technically been unnecessary and not time critical.

I tried to think of something to say to explain it, but Neritas stepped forward with the shield raised.

"This is a special kind of shield. A bit like the ones our guards carry but designed to work more with a red dragon's gifts. Scarlet's just charged it with magic that will hurt shadow catchers and combat the decay they use."

"That's fascinating."

"Sorry, I should have asked." His enthusiasm made me feel better. "It's powered with the magic of as many different colored dragons as possible. The more powerful and varied the magic in it, the more damage it does and the better it works."

"Ahhh, so you used a little of my magic? I understand now. Some of the guards reported feeling something similar when they went to rescue you in the classroom. Yes, I can see why this would have confused them and worried them without explanation."

"I try not to do it without permission, but I admit, it's becoming rather automatic for me to do it in certain situations."

"Such as being in danger and when you need to prepare for it." Griffin nodded as if this was a perfectly reasonable explanation, which made me feel a little better, but I still worried that I was getting far too used to being able to use magic and take it from the dragons around me. It felt good and made me stronger, and it was something I shouldn't get used to.

Before I could find out how Griffin felt about it and apologize again to him, everyone else arrived and I was ushered toward the door.

It was late in the day after everything else we'd been through, so everyone was eager to get on the road before it got too late. We wouldn't get to the gate that night. The place was too far away and we had too many moving parts and people to gather up still, but we'd visit it in the morning light of the next day.

It made sense to go then. The shadow catchers seemed to be least active in the morning, and I wanted to be at the gate when they were the most passive, if possible. It would make it easier to keep everyone safe. And I had no doubt that we would run into danger at some point if we followed this plan through.

I led the way down to the small piece of land that connected Detaris to the coast, finding Capricia already there with four other guards.

"Bigger team than last time." I saw the coldness in her eyes when she looked my way and was still not sure what I'd done to deserve it. We'd fought beside each other, saving each other and protecting the dragons with us, but something had changed once she'd got back.

I hoped she would be warmed again by going on another adventure, or at least reminded of what I was willing to do to defend those around me. Failing that, I was hoping to get her to see and admit that the gate needed our help to keep it sealed. She didn't have to like me, just believe in what I was trying to do.

With all of Capricia's guards, Griffin, and me and my five companions, we needed three cars. And I didn't doubt that Jace would have another carful. It was almost crazy to think of so many of us moving about, and I suspected that a bus was going to be a better option if these sorts of trips became more common.

Of course, I knew that most of the city elders wanted these trips to stop and were unlikely to ever condone regular trips, but I got the feeling this was going to be part of my life going forward. I seemed to need to sort out the world and I had a lot to figure out still.

The last few weeks, my focus had been stolen by the needs around me, and neither I nor Ben had put any more effort into translating Anthony's journal. So much was still locked inside it that I might need to know, and I'd had no time or opportunity to work with Ben to unlock it. I wasn't sure it would all be relevant now, as he hadn't worked out that I was the heir for sure. At least we didn't think so.

I tried to keep calm and focus on what I needed to do as more dragons flew around us and the more openly curious landed nearby to watch what we were doing. Others gathered around and some swept overhead. It took all my self-control not to flinch as dragons flew nearby. The pain and fear I'd felt at the hands of other dragons was far too fresh for me to not react.

Although I was in less pain now, I still hurt a lot and had to concentrate to hide that as well. I didn't want to show any of them weakness. I didn't trust them not to take advantage of it, even with an elder nearby.

"I want Griffin in a car with me." Capricia's tone showed she didn't expect any argument.

"I will ride with him as well," I replied, not hesitating to make my desire clear. "You can drive."

Capricia looked as if she might murder me at being told what to do, and Ben went to object, but my mother put a hand on his shoulder and whispered something to him no one else could hear.

"We'll ride with you as well." Neritas said, stepping forward as if he wanted to protect me.

"No, only four to each car, and one of the guards will also go with us."

"You and I are Griffin's guards," I shot back, not budging an inch. "Ben and Flick in the next car with two guards, and Sienna and Reijo in the final car with two more guards."

Flick didn't look happy either, but Griffin nodded.

"Perfect. That seems wise, given all the talents and the skills of our red dragons, to have one in the front of our convoy and the other in the rear. Well decided, you two. You make me very relieved to have such powerful dragons with me on my first outing in many, many years."

Griffin's words broke some of the tension, but I was still not sure how well my command would be received. A part of me didn't care. If it made us all safer, I was going to call the shots, and I needed dragons of lots of different colors with me. I almost insisted on more, knowing that the four of us weren't enough, really, but I trusted Flick and Ben to get to me swiftly, and Reijo would protect Sienna.

It was the best way I could think to split the group.

Despite Griffin giving his approval of the arrangements, I thought Capricia was going to continue to argue, but she directed her four guards to split themselves between the two other cars. Ben and Reijo opted to be the drivers for the other two, choosing cars they were familiar with and had driven before, and Capricia took the one she had used last time.

Grateful to be heading out, I got into the passenger seat beside Capricia before anyone could protest that too. She glanced my way and set her jaw, her lips firming into a line, but she didn't say anything and started the engine.

"Where are we meeting these *friends* of yours?"

I ignored the implied meaning behind her emphasis on "friends" and gave her directions. This was going to be a long journey if I let Capricia's disdain for what we were doing get to me. Instead, I focused on what was important. Griffin had agreed to come and see the gate for himself, and I appreciated his willingness to try to see what I did.

She wasn't happy about it, but Capricia was cooperating and taking her role as protector seriously. I appreciated that much from her and knew that in a fight with shadow catchers and handlers she would put everything aside to fight with me. She was the kind of dragon who put everyone's survival and her role as captain of the guard as her top priority.

As we drove, I tried to think of a way to break the tension, but a single glance at Griffin seemed to help. He was staring at the world around as if he'd never seen other cars and was fascinated by roads and people in general.

"When was the last time you left the city?" I asked him.

"Over a hundred years ago. There weren't even roads here. I've marveled at the cars in our little space for many years, but I thought we were rich beyond measure having so many. To come out here and see that there are many of them and ordinary humans use them to get to places… It's so far beyond how it used to be."

I grinned, wondering what it must be like to see technology advance so much. The world had changed a lot in a hundred years, and it would change a lot more in the next hundred. Would I be alive to see it? Dragons seemed to live a lot longer than humans and I was still young, though I was older than I'd realized.

Capricia spotted Jace's van before I did. The vehicle was off the road a few miles south of the city, and the dragon was chilling out by the driver's door. Although she frowned again and narrowed her eyes, my driver pulled over as well and turned the engine off.

I got out and Jace immediately nodded to me and sauntered over.

"Your Royal Highness. I hear that collective of dumbasses that call themselves the capital city decided to reject you as their sovereign."

"Something like that," I replied, as Griffin, Capricia, and Neritas came over. Everyone obviously heard what she said, as Neritas smirked, Capricia looked like she might growl, and Griffin raised his eyebrows.

It would have been almost amusing, if I wasn't worried about what Griffin thought and trying to thaw Capricia. Of course, the latter was likely to be difficult if I didn't know what had set her off in the first place.

As Griffin came closer, he smiled at Jace and shook her hand.

"Thank you for agreeing to meet us and take us to the gate. I appreciate that working with us isn't something you would normally do, and we're often considered on the other side."

"You're only on the other side because you put yourselves there. We just have different priorities, but we're still dragons and we still care about this planet and seeing it safe." Jace spoke matter-of-factly. Enough of her bravado was gone, and I was pretty sure this had an impact on Griffin.

He nodded in response and shook hands with the other dragons she'd brought with her as they all poured out of the van. I grinned as I saw Tim, Harriet, and Cios, and gave all three of them big hugs before being introduced to the extra two I didn't think I'd met before.

"These two remember you from the little bust-up we had with that handler the first time. Lerin and Peter."

I greeted the extra dragons, recognizing their faces now that they'd come closer and feeling the familiar connection of the magic they held. They'd been at the farmhouse, but there had been so many of them there and I'd been so exhausted that I hadn't had much capacity for remembering new people.

With the rest of the cars in my convoy pulling up and everyone else coming over to be introduced, it was a bit of a free for all for a few seconds. The guards were wary at first, but Capricia grew friendlier when Jace told her that she was grateful to have such an excellent dragon and warrior at her side again.

Of course, Jace knew nothing of what Capricia had been saying or doing since they'd last met, and I didn't want to interfere. Jace might help me thaw her after all. Although I tried to keep it casual, I threw in praise and appreciation for the dragons we had, and tried to turn the conversation toward our next matter: the plan for this trip.

"Forgive me for derailing us a little longer, but there's something about you, Jace," Griffin interrupted. "You seem familiar."

"I used to be in the city guard in Detaris. When I was younger. You were an elder even back then."

"Well, that makes me feel a little older than I'd like but that would explain it. At some point on this little mission of ours I'd like to hear about why you left. But forgive me, we have important matters to discuss. Like when we eat and sleep, and when we get to see this ever-important gate."

I nodded and smiled as Jace pulled out an old-fashioned map and spread it out over the front hood of the van. Something about Griffin's manner seemed to help. He was so enthusiastic and generally eager to get along and take an interest that eventually everyone warmed to him. I decided to learn from his example.

It felt as if being a red dragon naturally made me more of a hothead, as others accused my kind of, but I knew if I could temper it a little, it could be something I harnessed. Turning it into passion and drive rather than destructive anger would serve me better.

Jace marked on the map the position of the gate. It was already after dark now and we were going to want to sleep before we got too near.

As I expected, Jace decided to take us on a slightly different route, heading toward a campsite that was fairly out of the way and as close to the gate as any of us dared to get before dawn.

No one disagreed as she explained every step and made sure Capricia and her guards were on board with where they were heading as well as who would take guard duty and when.

Although I had some thoughts to share, I found most of

them had been anticipated and I had a feeling the rest would be argued with as riskier. I wanted to be more involved in protecting everyone, but I knew I would have to play my part if shadow catchers appeared, and I was still in a lot of pain. The time on my feet had made it worse.

"All right. If we have no more objections, questions, or suggestions, I think we're ready to move out. Red, I assume you and Capricia want to take the lead to the first target?"

I nodded as Capricia nodded and gave me a look that made it clear I would be the first to face any danger that appeared while we were awake.

"I'll take up the rear then." Jace swung herself back into the passenger seat of the van. Cios, as usual, drove her group.

I ushered my team back to their places, and within a minute we were on the road again, finally a full convoy with a complete plan. But I couldn't help wondering how much of it we'd be able to stick to and how much the demons of the world would derail us.

CHAPTER TEN

By the time I saw the late-night diner we'd been aiming for I ached all over and was struggling to sit and focus. I was exhausted and clearly more injured than I'd thought, despite all the healing my mother had managed to do. The road hadn't been in great shape either, and the ride had jolted me far more than I'd appreciated.

Although I'd tried to hide it, Capricia slowed as she came into the parking lot and gingerly parked.

"You look like shit, Scarlet," she said as she turned the engine off. "I guess you can't handle everything thrown at you as if it's nothing."

"Of course I can't. I'm not perfect." I was not sure if Capricia was speaking out of concern or mockery.

A part of me didn't care. We'd made it to the diner, and that meant I could sit and eat and not have to hold myself quite so straight and endure so much bumping around. I now wished I had found a place to sleep closer to this so that I wouldn't have to get back into a car as soon as we were done eating.

Before I had done more than open my car door and stand, Neritas was at my side, his arm slipping around me to help support me.

"I know you're trying to hide how much pain you're in," he whispered. "But you need to let us help you."

I frowned, not sure how to respond. He looked as if he was being more than a friend, and Flick's eyes went wide as he got out of his car and joined us. Neritas was trying to save my pride by appearing to be something else, but it wasn't a good impression to make.

Too much pain coursed through me, and I was too tired to argue, so rather than pull away I leaned into him, grateful for the support.

Flick came to my other side, and I decided to even things up a little and take the sting out of it for him by reaching out an arm, encouraging him to hug me in a similar manner.

If anyone else thought this strange, they didn't show it. Only the waitress at the diner looked at me as if I was a megaslut. It probably didn't help that all the burly guards from Detaris, plus Tim, Cios, Ben, and Peter all followed closely behind while Griffin, Jace, and Sienna talked about diners and what we were about to do in hushed whispers with Capricia bringing up the rear.

The waitress didn't seem to appreciate me asking for a table big enough for my whole party this late at night, but when Peter and Cios offered to move the tables for her and put them back when we were done, it seemed to soothe her anxiety and she showed us to an area where we could move tables and chairs and arrange them as we wished.

Griffin appeared to be fascinated by everything, especially the drink machines and appliances everywhere. The dragon city had similar items, but they were all magic powered, and he had thought a lot of the electricity-powered devices were made possible by the abilities of yellow dragons, not inventions of a human.

While we waited for our food, I gave a human science lesson on electricity and everything it had led to. It helped keep my mind off the pain and hunger I felt. Griffin wasn't the only one interested in listening—some of the guards leaned toward me as I spoke as well.

Capricia sat back, her focus on the door. I couldn't blame her, when she was the one in charge of the security of Griffin and all the other dragons from Detaris.

The diner was familiar. I was pretty sure we had eaten at it before, but I didn't recognize our waitress and she didn't seem to recognize us. I was grateful for that. The last thing I needed was someone who picked up on who we were.

As had become my habit when not in the city, I kept feeling out around us for signs of shadow catchers. I couldn't feel any, but I glanced at my mother a few times to check that she was calm as well. While I was tired and hurt, I wasn't going to trust myself entirely to feel any danger nearby.

Everyone tucked into the food with gusto, silence falling over the table for several minutes while we devoured the food that had been prepared for us. It took me longer to eat than I'd have liked. My arms ached, especially where they had been broken, and it almost made me give up, though I was still hungry.

Eventually we were all sat back, sated and able to

appreciate being dragons out in the world. Griffin was fascinated as I got the bill and Reijo paid. I offered, but he pointed out that all my money came from him anyway.

I didn't argue with his sound logic, but it felt weird to be reminded that I wasn't standing on my own two feet in that way. For a queen, I was pretty pathetic. Beaten up, trying to reign over an entire race who would rather ignore the real danger they were in than have a queen, and with no money or wealth of any kind. Just hunted and vilified.

Not wanting to feel any worse than I did, I tried to push the thoughts from my head. Instead, I focused on Griffin and the two guards flanking him who had never left the city before. With any luck, I was showing them that the human world wasn't so scary and had its benefits.

With the food so good, everyone full, and no hurry to be anywhere until the following day, no one seemed to want to move, but I couldn't shake my underlying fears. There had been too many occasions where I had outstayed my welcome and come to regret it. If I was in one place that was public enough for more than a couple of hours, I grew anxious.

This meal was no exception, and I was soon casting my mind outward to see if I could feel danger coming our way. For now, I felt nothing, but I couldn't quite relax either way. The aches I still had didn't help. Food had given me more strength to endure it, but it was making me tired.

"Okay, I think it's time we moved on," Capricia suggested once the bill was paid and it was clear that no one was going to leave without encouragement. "I don't know about any of you, but I want to sleep before we face whatever shitshow tomorrow might be."

Everyone got up to file out of the diner, and I was pretty sure that the waitress was glad to see us go. The place was empty except for our group. I left her a hefty tip, grateful I could at least do that.

We convened outside long enough that all the drivers could get the address for our next destination and make sure they knew where they were going.

"Why can't you all just follow me?" Capricia asked. "I know where we're going, thanks to Jace here."

"That may be true, but it's good for all of us to know," Jace replied, smiling a little too sweetly.

"Fine, but I'll be taking the lead either way."

"Wouldn't have it any other way. But you can relax once we get there. The whole place is perfectly safe. Dragon safe at that. No one is going to be bothering us."

I got the impression Jace had something magical there that would protect us. Sort of how Detaris could partially shield itself from shadow catchers and they didn't appear to find it easy to locate, plus the water it was surrounded by kept them from getting close via all but one route

Capricia didn't look impressed, and stalked off toward our car. For a moment I hesitated. This was proving a tense journey and I didn't want to get back into the car with her and have to endure more driving. Being able to sit and eat had allowed some of the aches and pains to fade, but I didn't doubt that this next part of the journey was going to make it worse again.

As the others went to their vehicles, Griffin and Neritas came to my side to head to our vehicle with me. Griffin was still grinning ear to ear, and Neritas slipped his arm around me again.

"Not much longer now, and you can rest." His voice was low, almost a whisper again, and I appreciated the care in what he was doing. Feeling as if I wasn't entirely alone facing all this was some comfort.

He walked me all the way to the passenger seat as Griffin got in the car. Soon I was sitting, hiding the flare of pain at getting down low and twisting into the car as best I could. Closing my eyes, I tried to do what I usually would when leaving a place or wanting to focus on something beyond my body, and felt outward for any sense of evil.

Being in so much pain made it a lot harder, but I controlled my breathing and zoned out from the car and all its distractions with more ease than normal. I didn't want to be there, and in some ways that made it easier.

Capricia pulled off, jerking the car and flaring more pain up my back and through both arms as I tensed and tried to brace myself. My eyes snapped wide as I felt something off to the west of us. I exclaimed and tried to concentrate again, but now that we were moving, I was in too much pain to get the same level of focus and reach out as far.

I swore, and Capricia glanced my way.

"What's got your panties in a bundle?" she asked, but I doubted she cared much about the answer.

"I think I felt something. Back the way we came."

"Not another one of your 'the shadow catchers are coming' premonitions. I'm getting pretty tired of them." Capricia continued to drive away.

"Pull over. I need to be sure."

"Nope, princess, we're not stopping and you're not in charge. We dealt with Fintar. That handler had been controlling everything. If you can feel anything now, I'm going to bet it's just a coincidence or fear playing tricks on your mind."

"That's not how this thing works."

"I don't care how it works. I'm not stopping this car again until we get to our little dragon hotel." Capricia flicked her gaze at me a couple more times, her face set and her expression clear.

I clenched my fists, ready to give her a piece of my mind about the danger we might be in, but Neritas placed a hand on my shoulder where Capricia wouldn't see it. The meaning was clear. I should let this one go.

Although I wanted to argue and insist, I settled back and tried to calm the nerves in my body and relax enough that the pain faded as much as possible. It wasn't easy when I couldn't be certain we were safe, but I needed to trust Jace to some degree. If she thought we would be safe wherever we were going, then I had to believe we would be.

So far, the dragon had been trustworthy and just as put out every time the shadow catchers had shown up. But we still didn't know how the monsters always found me. Fintar had been a good explanation about half the time, but *only* half the time.

If nothing else, I figured I would know if Jace was trustworthy after this night was through. When she'd given me her word that we'd be safe, if the shadow catchers found us here and caught on to us, I would see her reaction and know if she was pleased or not.

Of course, only Ben had been there every time, but I had seen the pain in his eyes when the shadow catchers had got Anthony and the surprise, fear, and determination with which he'd fought them. It wasn't Ben either.

As we drove east, I tried to stop myself thinking about that. It had never done any good to dwell on how the demons were finding me. It was a question I didn't have an answer to, and it never changed the decisions I needed to make. For the good of the world, I would keep taking risks and trying to find a way to unite the dragons.

Thankfully it was only another hour before we reached the address Jace had given Capricia. She turned down a small lane, but it was smoother than I was expecting, as if someone had laid fresh dirt down recently and packed it flat. It cut through a small, wooded area for half a mile before it revealed another body of water. A few hundred yards out in the middle of the lake was a large yacht.

I chuckled at the simplicity of it. Shadow catchers could come toward us, but they wouldn't get to us.

A small jetty held a couple of smaller motorboats on the end of tethers, and a dragon sat in one of them already. She looked up at us as we stopped, one of her hands on the rope that held her and the other boat in place as if she was trying to decide whether she should stay or cast off.

"At ease, Trisha," Jace said as soon as she got out of the van. "This motley crew is with me."

"When you said you were bringing a group to the boat, I didn't think you planned to fill her up to bursting. We're going to have to make two trips."

"Noted. Take the vulnerable and tired first and get them settled." Jace grinned and passed a rucksack toward Trisha.

The young dragon took it and motioned for others to join her. Cios went to helm the second boat and I ushered Griffin in that direction as well. No one else seemed keen to go, but Jace sent some of her guards as well, and Capricia encouraged my mother and Reijo to also get in the first transport.

Keeping Neritas and Flick with me, well aware that they would have protested me sending them off anyway, I considered what team would be best protection from the remaining dragons. I needed a dragon of each color if I was to have full control, but with Jace, Capricia and my two bodyguards, that left only needing to cover blue. Only Ben and Reijo were blue as far as I knew.

I wasn't sure I could have sent Ben off anyway. He was already coming close to me and looking me over for signs of exhaustion and pain. I smiled at him as if I were fine, but I wasn't sure he bought it. Either way, someone had to stay on shore, and as our best line of defense, it made sense for it to be me.

Capricia insisted on keeping one of her guards, and Jace kept Tim for good measure. I watched the rest head off in the small boats with all our luggage. It meant there would be more of us in the second wave, but it left space for all of our belongings in the first.

Although we'd left the demons behind us, I closed my eyes and focused on the feel of the area. I wanted to be sure we had time to get to the yacht. A fight in my current state didn't seem like a good idea, even with the backup I had.

Neritas seemed to sense my reluctance and stood close by the whole time, supporting me with his charged shield at the ready. I appreciated the seriousness of his attitude, but also feared for how committed he was becoming. I didn't want him to think a relationship beyond friendship was possible between us.

A small voice in my head tried to ask me if I'd consider it if I was free to be with anyone, but I pushed the thought away and scrutinized the area carefully.

Now I had time, support, and quiet, I could get my head in the right zone and be sure that no evil lurked ready to attack. Despite my state, I took the time to practice pushing out the area I could detect them in, wanting to figure out how to get better and further.

It was the one skill I didn't ever practice while in the city, as the shadow catchers were often far from my mind, but I had a feeling I'd need it over the next period of my life.

We stayed safe and the world around me remained calm until the boats came back for us and took us to the yacht as well. By the time we joined the others, the rooms had been divided up and everyone had a place to sleep and stow their luggage for the night.

There were two more dragons aboard, a skeleton crew, something that appeared to annoy Capricia, but their promise to have breakfast ready for us at dawn soothed her ruffled feathers and allowed me to walk away to get some sleep finally.

CHAPTER ELEVEN

I exhaled with relief as Mom finished moving the healing device over my body once more. A decent night's sleep and some more of the magic contained in the device had made a big difference to how I felt. There were still sore spots, and I didn't doubt that I would ache again by the end of the day, but I wasn't struggling as much as I had the day before.

The remains of breakfast sat on a plate beside me, a couple of crusts left of the vast quantity I'd been given. I'd slept through the entire night on top, and although it was early and we'd gone to bed late, I felt far fresher.

When I reached out with my mind and instantly felt the lurk of evil off toward the gate, I was grateful I was doing so much better.

No part of me doubted that I would fight shadow catchers today. They were the bane of my life outside the dragon city, and it seemed they had been drawn to me yet again. For now, however, they seemed to be keeping their distance.

I'd told Mom and the others about them, but while the

demons hung back, we were all getting ready to head out again. Griffin was clearly nervous, and Capricia's black guards who hadn't left Detaris before were trying to hide similar feelings, but they were the only ones who hadn't faced the shadow catchers yet.

All the others had done so at my side and seen me kill them as well. That gave a dragon a little more confidence than normal.

"Time to move out," I called a few minutes later after I'd checked my rucksack again and made sure I had everything I wanted.

We'd already discussed a plan for the day. If everything went well, we would be back at the city by nightfall, but if it didn't and we got separated or something else bad happened, such as being overrun by shadow catchers, we would come back to this yacht to make a new plan or call for support.

I noticed that this time the city hadn't given us one of the beacons to summon aid that Ben had used before. With Griffin in our midst, I'd have thought they would, but no one had mentioned it and I wasn't about to beg for support when any situation that would require it would be more dangerous for the dragons who responded than it was for me.

No one could help me now. I had to hold the line and save the day.

By the time I was on the deck of the yacht, the sky was much brighter with the sun just off the horizon and the colors on display brightening my mood. This was the time of the day I loved the best and when I felt the most alive. If a shadow catcher came for me now, I knew I could give it a good fight.

It was almost as if they could sense me and felt a good amount of fear, because as we moved to the shore, they dropped back and away from us. I gave my group the good news.

"I'm not sure it's something to get too excited about, Red. If they're hanging back, they are probably waiting for the right moment, event, or circumstance," Jace pointed out.

"We're going to the gate. If we don't assume that it's a trap, we're not being wise at all." I hadn't wanted to voice such a gloomy thought out loud, but I saw little point sugarcoating these sorts of things.

Griffin came closer, seemingly instinctively, but I put a hand on his shoulder and tried to smile reassuringly.

"I got there and back twice before and made sure I could handle everything they threw at me. We'll be okay as long as we keep moving and stay together."

This seemed to do a little more for him as we got in the cars in our designated groups from before. Once again, Jace had given everyone directions to our destination and the dirt parking spaces off the side of the road.

I thought I knew most of the way by now, but I didn't say anything, not wanting to get anyone lost or piss off Capricia more than necessary. She didn't appear to be in a good mood and had barely said more than a few words to any of us all morning. It made me a little worried that this trip wasn't helping to win her over, but I could understand how this was hard for her.

"Thank you for this," I offered once we were on the

road again and leading our convoy. "I know you want to be back at Detaris and guarding the city you love."

"You're damn right I do," she replied, but I saw her relax a little and it took some of the tension out of the air.

"You do a good job and have every citizen's gratitude," Griffin added as he gazed out the side window at the world passing him by. We were still out in the middle of nowhere and I was keeping a feel on the rough location of the shadow catchers.

It was strange to have them nearby and not be doing something about it, but we had to forge ahead and hope. Without a handler they might keep their distance, especially if they knew that I'd killed one recently.

As I had this thought I realized I didn't know if shadow catchers communicated between themselves or had sentient thought outside of being controlled by handlers. They appeared to have some sort of self-preservation—and a desire to hunt and kill me—but that didn't mean they were sentient or had anything remotely close to the human capability for thought.

Wolves could hunt and chase down their prey, but that didn't mean that a wolf pack would know that a person was a bigger threat for having killed another pack in the past. Would these demons be as unable to act in their own best interests?

I had no idea, but I got the feeling I was about to find out. So far, these shadow catchers being cautious was a sign that either someone else controlled them, someone who was capable of acting on the safe side, or the creatures knew who I was and weren't going to attack until the right moment.

As the minutes ticked by and the shadow catchers behind faded from my mind, I felt the ones ahead getting closer. I frowned, and Capricia picked up on it.

"What is it?" She glanced my way a couple of times before focusing back on the road ahead.

"We're traveling faster than the demons can. Catching up to them."

"Do you want me to slow down so we stay a similar distance between them all?"

I shook my head. "No. If this is a trap, I don't want to make it easy for them to gang up on us."

Capricia grinned at my words and put her foot down ever so slightly more. If nothing else, I was grateful that she was willing to put all the animosity and disagreements aside when it came to fighting shadow catchers and fighting with strategy and skill. And I knew it was what had won her over the first time.

We made a good team. And for the most part we had the same goals. Dragons like us were protectors. Keeping everyone else safe and unharmed was the reason behind most of our actions. We just had it fueling a different aim. I wanted to take what I thought were necessary risks to protect all dragons, and Capricia felt a greater tie to a particular city and keeping those dragons safe.

If I thought about it logically, I couldn't fault her reasoning. It was the role she had been trained for, and few of the dragons from different cities mixed.

With the convoy traveling a little bit faster, it was apparent that we were catching the shadow catchers ahead and they could feel us coming.

As we got closer, rather than getting in our way, they

parted to the sides and moved away from us in other directions. I let Capricia know and she frowned.

"If it was just a few of us and we had only experienced fighters, I'd suggest hunting them." Capricia glanced my way as she spoke, and I caught a glimpse of the anger in her eyes. She hated these creatures and her hatred of them was making me an ally against them. If nothing else, I was grateful for that.

Instead of hunting the creatures, we had to drive past them, however, and it increased my feeling of unease. It wouldn't take long for all the shadow catchers to group up behind us, and that meant that we were likely to have to face them as one large group, cut off from our safehouse.

On top of that, it wasn't much farther to the parking area we needed. Capricia almost overshot it, but she slowed right at the last second. Thankfully, everyone behind her had been following their own directions and had already anticipated the turning and slowed, or someone would have likely rear-ended us.

The parking lot wasn't empty—two other cars were parked in such a way that they could be driven away swiftly. I recognized both of them. We had more allies meeting us here.

As soon as I got out, Merrik stepped from the shadows under the trees. His dark skin had helped hide him before he'd moved. I smiled and went over to him. Alitas was with him, and two more dragons I didn't recognize.

Jace and Cios were also pleased to see them and ushered them over to meet the rest of our group. All my enthusiasm disappeared the moment I saw Capricia's face. She was glaring at Merrik as if he had just murdered her life partner and thought it was okay to be friends after that.

I looked between them, not daring to breathe, but Jace acted as if she hadn't noticed any of it and there was no problem. It was strange to watch but I was willing to sit back and let it play out for now. If it meant I could study everyone and have time to think, I wasn't going to rush to any decision.

"This is Merrik, captain of the previous honor guard," Jace said as some of the dragons came forward, eager to meet a dragon everyone had heard of.

"Technically, I'm still captain of the honor guard."

"A dishonor guard, more like. You betrayed the duty you swore to," Capricia growled, not hiding the anger she felt.

"I acted exactly as my king commanded, even if not everyone understood it or why I did what I did."

"And Merrik was pardoned and had his case heard in the elders' chamber, Capricia." Jace stepped between the two of them and faced off with the city captain as well. The tension swelled. This wasn't how I'd imagined any of this going.

This didn't appear to be the first time Merrik had faced an angry outburst, however. He stayed calm, lifting his hands slightly and he moved past Jace to be closer to Capricia, almost apologetically.

"I've always taken my role very seriously, but because of it and my loyalty to the king, I can't always explain every action I take and why. But I assure you, as I did the elders, that I have always done my duty and obeyed the commands I was given. I was also never demoted, and the position outlasts the monarch's death. My duty automatically transfers to the heir, and I understand that's…" Merrik's words trailed off as his gaze roved over the group and Mom came closer. "Sienna!"

Merrik bowed and swept his whole torso down low as he did. It was an unexpected show of reverence, when the burly guy had been so much more stoic before.

As he straightened, my mother went over to him, and her eyes lit up as she took his hands.

"It's so good to see you again, Merrik. I know you have done and continue to do everything you can for the monarch and the royal line. I have no doubt that you followed all your commands to the letter because I witnessed it with my own eyes. You have my respect, and my recommendation is that you continue to serve Scarlet as the captain of her honor guard. She is the heir and the rightful queen."

Merrik nodded and bowed a little again before looking at me.

"I didn't say this officially the last time I was here, but I pledge my allegiance to you as the heir to the throne and my queen. I would consider it the highest honor to serve yourself as I did your father. Your safety, well-being, and every need of yours will be my highest priority and I will ensure that you are not in more danger than necessary." Merrik got down on one knee in front of me and lowered his head.

Not sure what to do in response to this, but worried I'd missed my cue and committed some elaborate social faux pas, I looked toward my mother. If she knew of something specific I was meant to do or say, she didn't share it, merely broadened her smile and encouraged me to focus back on Merrik.

"Thank you," I said to let him know he was appreciated and buy myself time to think.

Everyone looked at the two of us in silence. It was awkward, but I wasn't going to let it get to me if I could help it.

"The honor would be all mine," I replied eventually. It was a cliché, and I was struck yet again by the oddness of having people pledge themselves to guard me, serve me and all sorts of other related things.

All I wanted to do was be a normal person, fly and spend time with the family I was gaining through awesome friends or the mother I had found. But some people kept telling me I was a queen, and others kept attacking me for it.

"Okay, this is not happening." Capricia stepped forward. "She's just told Detaris and everyone in it that she wasn't going to be queen. I haven't come out here for her to build up more support just to change her mind again. If this is what this trip is about instead, then I'm going back to the city and I'm taking my guards with me."

"That's not what this is about." I was stunned by the vehemence in her voice. How could this have gone so wrong so swiftly? "Merrik and these dragons with him have been guarding the gate in the absence of an heir. Doing what they can to keep us safe. I didn't come here looking for anything I haven't already got."

"Forgive me, please. I don't intend to get in the way of why you're here. And I won't be pressuring Scarlet to do anything she does not wish to do. It is news to me that she doesn't wish to be queen, but either way, the gate is in danger and only Scarlet can channel the power of the dragon race to strengthen it." Merrik tried to talk to Capricia, but she walked off part way through his statement. He carried on so everyone else would hear him, speaking clearly.

I wasn't sure it was going to do much good. Capricia seemed to be finding every reason she could to hate this mission. But I needed Griffin to go to see the gate, whether she wanted to be supportive or not.

I wanted to tell the city guard captain where to shove her opinions, and I clenched my fists in anger at having her assume the worst of me all the time. Somehow, though, I stayed where I was and let her walk away.

CHAPTER TWELVE

It took me several seconds to notice that everyone was staring at me. All of them expected me to fix the problem, and not one of them was going to say anything to Capricia to get her to come back and take this mission seriously.

As ready to smack her as talk to her, I walked toward the car that Capricia was loading her stuff back into.

"I don't want to hear it. I don't trust a word out of your mouth," she snapped before I could speak. It didn't help my determination to not use violence as a solution, but I looked back at the others and held myself back for their sake.

"Honestly, I haven't come here to say anything other than remind you that Griffin wants to see the gate and that you also swore an oath, just like some people are doing to me. You swore to protect him. If you plan on walking away after all that—not to mention you and I both know that there are shadow catchers out there—I don't know why you insist on calling yourself a protector."

She looked up at me and swore.

"I know," I said. "It's shit having to do something you don't want to because it's what someone else wants or expects, isn't it?"

This earned me a raised eyebrow.

"Can I get one honest answer before I commit to walking up that trail with a bunch of demons on my ass and their boss buried in the ground ahead of me?" she asked.

"Sure. I think we both need a little straight talking."

"Do you want to be queen?"

"That's complicated, but in essence, no. I don't want to rule. But if it keeps Earth and the dragons and humans I care about safe, then yes, every ounce of my strength will go into fighting to be queen."

"So, you haven't given up on the throne?"

"I honestly don't know the answer to that. If I can get this gate protected and strengthened without taking the throne, then great. I don't need it. I don't *want* it."

Capricia studied my face, but then she looked over at the others and I knew that what I'd said had made little difference.

"Look, I didn't want to do a lot of things, but I have shadow catchers hounding me everywhere I go, and I have to keep fighting them, and I've got a bunch of dragons who want me to save the world and be queen. Whether we can agree on me being queen or not, can you really take the chance that you might be wrong on the world being in danger?"

"That might be the first sensible question you've asked in months." Capricia pursed her lips but relaxed her shoulders.

"I'll accompany our elder to this gate. But know I do it under severe protest at the company you keep, Red."

"I know. But if nothing else, try to consider them as extra power supply for me to charge weapons and shields if we do get attacked. To some degree, the more the merrier."

Although Capricia didn't say anything to this, I got the impression she considered it to be another decent point and it helped her come back with me.

As we rejoined the group, I didn't draw attention to her but motioned for Merrik to lead the way. I knew this trek wasn't going to be easy and I was once again prepared for the strange resistance that built as we got closer to the gate.

While we traveled, I also kept feeling outward for the unsettled areas the shadow catchers and handlers could make in my mind. I was grateful that I could feel them more easily and farther out. I felt the gate ahead of me, sooner than I had felt it before. Even without much practice lately, I was growing in skill and sensitivity.

I could feel the shadow catchers keeping their distance still, some of them following and some of them seeming to hold stationed points along the route we were trekking. Along the way I counted up all the ones I thought might be individuals, trying to get an estimate of what I was walking into, but when it got to over twenty, I wondered if it was better not to know.

They outnumbered us considerably, but with any luck they wouldn't reach us all at once. And I had fought so many before with less aid. Of course, I'd had a building I could defend, and this time I was out in the wilderness, but I tried not to think about that.

I soon had more pressing concerns anyway. The group was slowing as the oppression grew, and I could feel it weighing down my body as well. It was a strange sensation, a mental weight that was so heavy that the body felt it. It made me want to shrink my area of focus.

In some ways, however, it was easier, and I noticed that Merrik and the guards with him seemed to be less impacted as well, even less so than me. Their heads remained upright while the rest of the group was looking down. Would the feeling of trudging through treacle get easier to bear or lose its intensity with time? They had all been here many times and patrolled the area. This walk was nothing new to them.

I wasn't sure how each member of our group was affected, and I didn't want to draw attention to the negative in case they reinforced it in each other, so I kept quiet and studied them.

Griffin was struggling, and I shifted to walk alongside him and slip one of my arms under his.

"This is quite a long trek. I'm sorry, I should have given you more warning or brought some of those walking sticks with us or something." I tried to make light of the difficulties.

"A walking stick would definitely be a useful aid for a weary old dragon such as myself." He smiled up at me, but I saw a sadness in his eyes that the expression didn't take away.

It made me wonder what mental demons everyone else had to battle to get closer to the gate. Did they have similar thoughts to mine? I almost always worried that I was taking the wrong route, that I wouldn't be believed even once people saw the problem for themselves, and the thought that plagued me most—that I was an awful leader of any kind and would never be worthy to call myself a queen.

"A stick can probably be arranged," Merrik offered a moment later as the group halted to take a break. I thought we were a quarter of the way along the path at most, and it was only going to get harder.

I caught Jace's eye, and she frowned at the pause as well. She was faring a little better than some of the others, but generally also looking weary. The whole group expressed interest in having large sticks as Merrik returned with a branch that must have fallen off a tree for Griffin.

The elder took it with a grateful smile and a nod, and a few of the others looked for their own. The dragon guards looked concerned as the group spread out a little, but I reached out with the magic connection I'd been holding to all of them and found I could tell where they all were.

"We should get moving again as soon as we can," Merrik suggested, one of the few now remaining on the path with me, Griffin, and Jace.

"As soon as they've all got a stick, I guess." I shrugged, prepared for this to take all day if it needed to. We could always go back to the boat at the end instead of back to the city.

"You seem very calm about them spreading out. It is easy to get lost in these woods." Merrik studied me for a moment as if he were curious about my strategy. Instantly, I felt the stab of fear that he was judging me as a leader and finding me wanting.

"I can feel them all at the moment. They're all safe

enough. The shadow catchers are also hanging back. If any of them get too far away or too close to danger, I'll know immediately."

Although I hadn't directly lied, I did give myself a more confident-sounding attitude than I truly had. I was concentrating on the connections I had and feeling out for danger as much as I could in case something went wrong. Thankfully, the first few were already returning.

Flick came back particularly pleased to have found a branch that was significantly straighter than most, but instead of keeping it for himself, he switched it out for Griffin's, giving the struggling elder a better prop.

"Bless your young heart." Griffin patted Flick on the shoulder. That single kind act lifted the mood of the rest of the group who witnessed it, but I noticed Capricia still looked gloomy at the back.

Ben was the last to return. I'd worried about him and how long he was taking, and I released a long breath when I could finally feel him coming back to us. I'd dropped most of the other connections to concentrate on the one I had with him by then as I'd felt it stretch over a longer distance.

"Do we need to send out a search party for him?" Griffin asked not long later.

I shook my head and looked toward where I knew he was.

"No. He's on his way back and safe enough." Many of the others who hadn't been there to witness me telling Merrik that I could sense them all exchanged glances.

Mom smirked at everyone, knowing what I could do, but neither she nor I explained this time. I didn't want everyone to know what I was capable of. Capricia and her guards were now a large unknown in my mission.

When Ben finally did rejoin us, he had two sticks, one in each hand. I opened my mouth to tease him about being an old man who needed two when he brought one of them over to me.

"I knew you'd stay here and keep a lookout for demons and us being safe, so I got you one as well." He met my gaze with a determined nod that spoke of his desire to make sure I was okay too, no matter how hard this was on him.

"Thank you." My voice was barely above a whisper and I had a lump in my throat. It was a simple gesture, but after all the expectations, anger, and accusations that had come my way, that simple kind act made a huge difference.

Merrik wasted no time taking the focus back on him and insisting on leading the way forward. Internally I thanked him for doing so. I was eager to keep going and make it to the gate now that everyone seemed to have recovered a little.

The gain we made didn't last long, however. Soon everyone was leaning hard on the walking sticks and panting. I felt hot and sweaty as the sun rose in the sky and beat down on us in a more open section of the path. Normally I would have enjoyed walking along in the sun with friends and surrounded by the beauty of a natural forest. Today wasn't a normal day, though.

Although Griffin now had a good stick, he was struggling again. Delphin came to his rescue this time, walking alongside him and talking in quiet voices of times gone by.

It freed me up to move back to the rear of the group near Capricia. The city gate guard was looking surlier, with her brow furrowed and her eyes dark with anger the farther we went.

"This is not my idea of fun," she remarked a few minutes later.

"It's not anyone's." I felt my stomach knot with anticipation that she was about to cause another fuss.

"This had better be worth it. Whatever this gate looks like and you want to show us in person, it had better be the proof that you've been claiming it is."

"You'll have to decide that for yourself. But I know what it should look like according to the stories and what it looks like now, and I know that it's getting worse." I shrugged again. This strange nonchalance was better than any worries or anxiety over the future and helped keep the oppressive weight of the gate's influence from impacting my decision-making. The less I cared about anything or reacted emotionally, the easier it seemed to be.

Capricia glared at me, but I ignored the look. Thankfully she wasn't the one driving this group forward, and she was taking my reminder that she swore to protect Griffin to heart.

The next hour saw us get about two-thirds of the way there. Everyone had needed to stop twice more since getting our sticks, and the distance between pauses had gotten smaller.

"There's something about this thing, isn't there?" Griffin asked. "I don't normally feel this bad when I go for a walk."

"It doesn't want you to get close," Merrik explained. "And it wants you to despair while nearby. To give up and let it win."

"Try not to think about it." Jace looked back toward Capricia. "And try not to dwell on anything negative in your heart. It can twist things in ways that leave a mark or an impression longer than you think."

Although I knew this comment was directed at the city captain, I saw others nod and try to raise their heads and walk on with the knowledge that they were facing the enemy. Maybe I should have said something sooner?

I exhaled, trying to also combat my negative thoughts and not let them get to me. It was easier said than done, but I knew I could resort to counting my steps and focusing on a number if nothing else worked.

We'd gone a few hundred more yards when Capricia growled and stopped.

"The rest of you keep going. We'll catch up," I instructed them. Thankfully, enough of the group did so, and the guards and Griffin hesitated only briefly.

"You don't command all of them. I do," she insisted as I drew closer, keeping her voice down. She flicked her eyes over my shoulder. Neritas held his shield in one hand and his stick in the other, making it clear that he wasn't going ahead without me.

"I don't command them all and neither do you." I fought to keep my voice even. "We both protect them. But that means we have to be stronger than they are. So if they can keep going, then so can we."

"You're forgetting. I don't want to keep going. I couldn't care less about seeing this gate or giving you any kind of proof. I already know that you're an arrogant moron."

I exhaled as Neritas rolled his eyes, an expression he didn't rise to often.

"Think what you like of me, but I shouldn't have to remind you yet again that you swore to protect some of these people and they're walking into danger without you."

"Oh, shove that shit where the sun doesn't shine. I don't have to protect anyone who walks into danger willingly." Capricia turned to walk away.

"Are you really this weak?" Neritas asked. His voice was calmer than mine or Capricia's, but with a commanding presence to it I hadn't expected before.

"Weak? You're calling me weak? I'm not stupid."

"The enemy doesn't want you approaching the gate and you're the only one succumbing to his mind games. He whispers in all our heads, Capricia, not just yours. You're the captain of the guard in the largest, most powerful dragon city in the world. You should be stronger than this. Strong enough to see it to the end whether you want to or not."

It was my turn to be impressed by the logical reasoning of someone else, but I didn't think Capricia appreciated it. Her face was an angry snarl that made me wonder if she was about to attack Neritas. Slowly, I moved my hand to the sword at my belt, hoping that I wasn't about to have to use it on a fellow dragon for the first time.

"I don't like you either, Neritas, but if you think I'm weak you're mistaken. I'm no fool."

"Which would you rather appear to be? You go back—you look weak. If you continue on with us, there's only a chance you'll be a fool. But no more a fool than the rest of us for believing there's something to see."

Capricia growled again, but she stormed past Neritas to catch up with the rest of the group. At first, I didn't move, feeling so exhausted that I thought I might pass out. Neritas slipped his arm around me, concern on his face.

"You're hiding how difficult this is well, but I get the feeling that you're being hit harder than any of us." He helped me take the first step and then another.

"I've faced it before. Twice. It gives me an advantage." I wasn't sure it was true, but an element of hope lay in my words. Either way, after his speech, I had no choice. I had to keep going, because I knew that of the two, I would also rather find I was in a group of fools than that I was too weak to see something through that I had started.

CHAPTER THIRTEEN

As we caught up with the group, I was dismayed to find how slowly they were moving, almost all of them were panting under invisible weight. Alitas and Merrik looked at me as if hoping I had some bright ideas, but I was pretty sure that anything I said would only anger Capricia at this point and splinter the group again.

"The demon behind the gate is a difficult one to fight against," Sienna told us. "But you should all be proud of yourselves for getting this far while locked in battles in your mind and with a body that feels as if it might fail you at any moment. Scarlet's father taught me several things that I have found helpful in approaching the gate in the past."

Griffin stepped closer to my mom as everyone paused again. She smiled and placed a hand on his shoulder.

"Close your eyes for a moment, all of you, and search your minds for a happy memory with someone you love. Imagine that person you love." She paused as she waited for all of us to comply.

Although I hesitated at first, I noticed everyone was doing it, even Capricia, and decided it couldn't hurt to join in. I closed my eyes and imagined some of my favorite moments with Anthony.

"Once you have that person firmly in your head, imagine that they're waiting for you at the end of this path and that they're cheering you on to reach it. Keep telling yourself whatever they would to encourage you. That you can do this. That it's just a matter of your mind over your body and you can win that fight, and know that when you do get to the end, you'll be the stronger for it."

As my mother spoke these last few words, I understood. She had hit the nail on the head, the reason it got easier for those who walked the path many times. You knew you could, because you'd done it before. The resistance wasn't any less.

"I also find it helps to not look too far ahead and think about how much farther you have to go. Be in the here and now and focus on putting one foot in front of the other. That's the only way to get there." Alitas spoke softly but he held everyone's attention.

By the time he and my mom were done talking about their techniques, the group was ready to carry on, and this time we managed to keep the pace fast enough that I also had to concentrate on putting one foot in front of the other and imagining Anthony at the other end cheering me on to find him.

Although he had been fairly softly spoken and didn't talk much, it was enough that I found it easier to keep going and before I knew it, we were most of the way along the path, with a few hundred yards to go.

When the group stopped, I exhaled with frustration I couldn't put into words. Then I looked far enough forward that I understood why. Once more, the gate's influence had crept out, and more of the forest was gone, decayed into nothing.

I slowly moved past the group, wanting to cry at how much natural beauty would now be gone if this happened all the way around.

"It's bigger," I said, not sure what else to say.

"It always is. A few inches a day now, and I think it's getting faster," Merrik confirmed my fears.

"This is all the gate's doing?" Griffin asked.

"The demon's doing… Or if you like, the gate's failing to prevent from happening."

I reached out to connect to all of their magic again, now that I felt I had the strength to do so.

"May I use your magic to show you something?" I asked, looking at them all and waiting until I had their attention.

Most of them nodded, although I noticed that Capricia did so only when the others had. She still wasn't convinced, but I had no idea how much more it would take to get her to see the truth.

I turned and reached for Neritas, who had the ability naturally and didn't need to draw on other dragons to heal the land. Delphin came forward on the other side and we healed the ground outward, pushing back the decay and growing plants, and making the grass and moss grow back over the land.

Maintaining it wasn't easy, and I struggled to keep it going as everyone watched.

"Okay, I think that's enough," I said when the area was wide enough for all of us to step out into. "Just hold it there."

I walked with them, encouraging everyone else to follow, but still drawing on their magic a little to help Neritas and Delphin hold the ground. It was something I hadn't known how to do in the same way the last time I was here, but I felt confident now and we all walked out into the gate's direct influence.

At first it was like walking through treacle, an almost invisible barrier on the edge, but then it was easier. Something about being there felt wrong, however. If we had felt downtrodden and weary coming closer, this was more like an anxiety that nothing was quite right. An almost madness.

"I can't see the gate," Griffin commented. "We should be able to see the covering and the intricate stonework and carvings that support it.

"It's so far away that it can't be seen from here." Unlike the first time I was here, I also couldn't see the tree line on the other side anymore. The circle of decay was now too large.

"Don't the lore books say that the gate was in a circle of grove trees and a secure area that had magic wards and all sorts?" a guard asked.

"Yes," Griffin replied. "We should be able to get right up to it."

"If it was fully powered, we would be able to. But it's weakening and the demon it holds is influencing everything, making it harder and harder to get to him to seal the gate up again."

"What will happen if this runs unchecked?" Harriet asked in a small voice.

I'd assumed she had seen this before, but I realized that wasn't the case from the open-mouthed expression on her face and the tear trailing down her cheek.

Alitas turned to her. "He'll break free. And he'll try to enslave the world, just as he did millennia ago. If you think our troubles with shadow catchers and handlers and all manner of other demonic creatures are bad lately, just wait. The dragons who guard the gate talk of the old times when all of them roamed free, and we don't forget."

His voice carried a mix of emotions, but most clearly disdain that any of the others could let it get this bad and not be worried about it. I could understand the anger and his desire to see something done about it.

Capricia looked around at it all, but her expression was unreadable. Whatever thoughts she had locked in her head, she kept out of the limelight. I wanted to ask her what she thought, but Neritas was struggling to hold the area of ground and I knew that we needed to back up a little again.

Soon we were back on the edge of the decayed area. The section we had healed was rapidly growing older, dying, and rotting before our eyes. Although I had seen it before, it was still shocking to watch, and I didn't think the feeling of being repulsed by it would ever stop happening. It was disgusting and wrong and I wanted to make it better right away.

"I don't mean to be pedantic, but this doesn't prove one very important point," Griffin stated.

"What point?" Jace almost scoffed.

I gave her a look that tried to tell her this wasn't the

time to be antagonistic, but Griffin didn't seem to mind and tilted his head to the side briefly as if thinking about how best to phrase it.

"This is clearly concerning and clearly a problem. But getting worse? We would have to come again to see how bad it is."

"Not necessarily. If you can show a little patience and are willing to wait a short while, we can probably prove it is moving and getting worse. Would that be enough for you?" Alitas' question was genuine.

"I'm willing to take any offer to understand that you're willing to give." Griffin again took some of the tension out of the air with his enthusiasm, and it helped me feel a little more positive about convincing the elder.

Alitas held his hand out for a stick. I gave him mine before anyone else could hand theirs over. With a small knife he made several fine notches on it and showed it to Griffin and those closest to him. My mom, Reijo, Harriet, Tim, and one of the city guards all leaned in to see.

"See that these are relatively evenly spaced and there are ten of them. I will put it down in the decay with the tenth right on the edge of the decay and the rest out toward us. If you can wait a short while, you will see it take the others." Alitas studied their faces in turn, getting a nonverbal assent from each of them.

I didn't know exactly how long this would take, but I got the impression it would be a while. I found a fallen tree log to sit on. My pack was heavy, and my legs ached after all the walking.

I broke out some of the snacks I'd stuffed in the side pockets and munched. A lot of the others followed suit and we began the strangest mid-morning picnic beside the rotting, decaying land while we all waited to see what would happen next.

Here again, a voice said in my head, making me jump.

I looked around, but no one had noticed me move and no one was looking at me. I knew that none of them had spoken. It wasn't them. It was something far worse. Something beyond the gate. It had spoken to me once the first time I was here, but I didn't want to talk to it and had ignored it.

What an interesting set of company you keep, Princess.

Queen, I couldn't help but think as he finished talking.

Not yet. You've not been crowned. That's why you carry it in that pack on your back and keep it hidden. You know that it's not really yours and you shouldn't ever wear it. Not even a pure red. Close, but not quite.

I exhaled, thinking of Anthony as I had earlier and hoping it would help me focus and ignore the voice. It was trying to get to me. That much was obvious, but it was hitting a little too close to home for me to be able to listen to it with confidence, and I didn't want it to think it was working.

"Raisins?" Reijo asked a few seconds later, holding out a small packet that had several handfuls missing already. I wasn't a fan of the sugary dried fruit, but the small, normal interaction was a welcome distraction from what was going on inside my head.

I munched on a few slowly and passed the packet on. Several of the snacks were circulating among the group, and it was nice to see everyone getting along for the moment, a common need and a rest in a slightly dangerous place enough to bring them together, if for only a short while.

The demon beyond the gate might not have been impressed with who sat in front of me, but I was, and I didn't doubt that they were powerful dragons in their own right. I had pulled magic from all of them and they hadn't seemed to care, with the exception of the two who had been straining to hold back a demon with me.

One thing was sure: getting to the gate was going to require a lot of green dragons, and with each passing day it was going to get a little harder. If we weren't careful, it was going to become too difficult and the entire dragon race wouldn't be strong enough to make it through. At least, that was how it felt sometimes. But then I remembered that dragons had put the demon there in the first place.

I thought back to the last large encounter with the shadow catchers. Humans had helped. I'd had to make their bullets magic to do any damage, but humanity was at the stage that if the worst happened and the demon broke free, dragons and humans alike would likely join the fight.

I held onto that thought as I tried to sense for danger again. The voice was quiet for now, but I could almost feel the darkness on the edge of my mind. It made me wonder if it was difficult for them to feel deeper and ask me questions. If it took energy.

All of this was unknown, and I couldn't tell the group that I was hearing voices I thought were from beyond the gate. With a few of them, I was already walking on thin ice. I wasn't about to make it worse.

After about an hour of eating, resting, and gentle conversation, none of us wanted to be close to the decayed area or even look at it. I got up and went over to the stick. Griffin and Jace joined me.

I counted the notches up. There were only eight visible. The ninth and tenth had been swallowed by the decay.

"It's definitely moving."

"Are you sure that nobody moved the stick?" Capricia asked. I imagined Neritas rolling his eyes again while I simply straightened back up and looked at Griffin to see his reaction to such a question.

"Nobody moved it. We were all sitting a really long way away from it and I kept an eye on it when Red got closer. Griffin was there next and I'm sure he can say the same thing."

"Yes, I'm satisfied, Capricia, although I appreciate you wanting to be sure. It is the decay. It is creeping outward and that is something of great concern, no matter the reason."

I felt something on the inside of me unwind at hearing this. I'd convinced one of the elders that it was true, and I was grateful that I wouldn't be fighting this battle in Detaris alone anymore.

Before I could suggest he take some photos or whatever evidence he thought he might need, Capricia grabbed her pack, slung it onto her back and stomped off back down the trail, the way we'd come.

"It's not safe to go off alone," Merrik called after her, but she stuck up her finger at him and carried on. I considered going after her, but Ben and Jace stopped me as well.

"She's had a stick up her ass about this from the beginning. Let her go." Ben looked me in the face. "She needs to do her own thing and you can only stop someone from doing what they think is best so many times before you have to let them try and learn for themselves."

Although I recognized the wisdom in Ben's words, I got the feeling I was going to regret her stubbornness and decisions. For some reason, she hated everything I stood for.

CHAPTER FOURTEEN

Griffin was clearly concerned, and I had to reassure him that Capricia knew the way. In the end, Delphin volunteered to take another of the gate guards and keep their distance but make sure that she got to the cars okay. A city guard asked to go as well, and I approved the idea.

While I wasn't happy that Capricia was being so difficult about our mission, I still wanted to make sure she was safe, and there were a lot of shadow catchers out there. I didn't want anyone to get hurt or die because they disagreed with me.

"This is something of great concern, and I feel as if we should try and do something while we're here," Griffin said. "I've come all this way and I feel as if I need to get as much information as possible to give the elders. Is there any way that we can get closer and check on the gate and its state? If I can see that it's broken or weaker or…"

Griffin looked as me as his voice trailed off and I moved to the edge of the decay again. I didn't like the idea of going farther, but everyone left with me was looking at me as if they expected me to have answers.

"It would require the magic of all of us, but if we tried to generate a narrow channel, we might be able to get closer. But Delphin was one of the green dragons whose powers we would need to achieve that."

"There are others in the area who guard the gate and keep the shadow catchers from driving us away." Alitas bowed to me. "With your permission, I would signal them."

I didn't want to summon others to me, but we had to try to see the gate for ourselves if I was going to prove this. If I didn't, and the elders reacted similarly to Capricia, I would regret it. And this way, I also made it clear that I also wanted answers and to heal the land.

It was going to be tough, but it was the only way I could proceed.

While I waited, I encouraged everyone to rest again. I half expected the shadow catchers to attack while we spent so long there, but they kept at bay and Alitas came over to me as soon as he'd finished sending his message to summon more green dragons to us.

"You seem tense and keep looking around. Are there demons we should be worried about?" He kept his voice low so that the others wouldn't hear.

"There are demons out there, but they're keeping their distance. I'm worried that if we do this and drain all of our magic merely getting to the gate, we won't be able to get out of here without losing someone. Fighting shadow catchers on top of everything else… There's a lot of them."

He nodded but didn't appear to be worried.

"If it changes, let me know. There are other ways out of

here that we can try if necessary. Not all of them are well maintained, but your father showed me something once and told me to use it in an emergency."

Gratitude filled me at his words. Having a backup plan, even if it was a bit of an unknown, was a huge weight off. The safety of everyone in my party was my responsibility, but I had to weigh it against the need to unite the dragons and save the entire world. It made me think of one of those philosophical questions that no one wanted to actually have to answer in real life.

We had to wait another half an hour or so for more green dragons to find us, by which point I thought Capricia would be back at the cars, assuming nothing had happened to her or the guards I sent out after her. They were too far away now for me to feel them properly, but I hadn't detected any danger before I'd lost her presence in my mind.

The three guards saluted Alitas and then me. No hint of anything but respect came from them. It meant it was crunch time and I had to figure out the best way to get us to the gate.

"Okay. I know all of you would like to see this in the flesh and have your proof for your respective groups, but I don't know if I can take all of you with me," I said once I'd thought about the problem.

"When you draw on the magic in all of us and we're all here because we're powerful dragons who've either sworn to serve you or are leaders in our own way, you can't afford for us not to join you. You need all our magic. You just need more green right now." Jace set her jaw, but I saw the twinkle in her eyes. She had a point and she knew it, but she wasn't expecting an argument, and she wasn't as confrontational as she might appear.

Appreciating her manner over Capricia's by a long way, I tilted my head to the side and thought for a moment. I looked back out over the decayed area. It wouldn't be easy to move a bigger group, but if I was careful how I did it and worked with the other green dragons, it could work.

"Okay. We'll all go. But we'll all need to stick close together and I'm leading the way with half the green dragons at the front and the rest spread out through the group."

"I recommend we go in twos and march like an army at the best pace our dragons can sustain," Alitas put in.

A single nod from me gave him the free rein he needed to organize the group, and everyone eagerly cooperated, letting him line them up and suggest walking buddies for everyone.

"We will need to keep together, keep an eye out on the pair in front and behind, and try to pace ourselves so we keep our group area small but move as fast as we can," Alitas was saying when Delphin and another gate guard returned.

"Capricia?" I asked.

"She's waiting in the car and safe. I've left the others to keep an eye on her," Delphin replied.

"Good." Alitas gave the guy a pat on the shoulder. "We're going to the gate, and you're a green dragon, so you're going to help us get there."

I stifled a grin at the way the older dragon commanded someone he clearly also considered a friend. Although it was a relief to hear that Capricia was safe and had been allowed back to the car by the shadow catchers in the area, I was most grateful that we'd gained another green dragon to help us.

As soon as the group was reassembled, slotting him in near the front as he was one of the more powerful dragons we had, I focused on feeling out for them all again. It was difficult to ignore the feeling of dread and unease that the gate itself created when I opened myself up to the shadow catchers, magic, and everything else I could sense.

I'd asked Mom if it was something that could be broken down into parts and controlled individually. If I could connect to others and be aware of them without being more aware of the demons nearby. But if there was a way, she didn't know how to do it. Opening up to magic and everyone connected would let everything in, it seemed.

With everyone else ready to go, I got the green dragons started, using my abilities to help channel magic to them but also to aid in the task. My mother did the same near the back of the group, making sure that the green and safe area we were creating didn't fall into decay before the rest of us could get through it.

It felt strange to step out again, but I was more prepared for it this time and pushed past the wall. Almost immediately, the presence of the entity behind the gate was stronger, as if I had walked into its domain. The influence it wielded could clearly push beyond the point where I had heard it, and it had the ability to make people dread getting up to the edge of the decay, but this was a different level.

Trying to focus on the simple task of channeling magic and controlling the land underfoot, I ignored how it felt as much as possible. Neritas walked beside me, his face set as he strode ahead. Alitas was right behind him, and another green dragon I didn't know behind me. It was the best arrangement we could achieve when many wanted to keep me safe.

Are you coming to see me, Princess? the voice taunted as we got about fifty yards in. I ignored it and the way it emphasized *princess*. Enough to make me notice, but subtle enough that I questioned whether it was intentional or not.

I wasn't playing mind games.

As we went farther, a weight seemed to settle in my heart, stronger than before. It was a deep despair that made me want to stop and give up. It wasn't the same as the fear earlier. It didn't make me want to turn around and go the other way, so much as stop and let the decay consume me.

But I wasn't giving in.

"Remember to focus on what matters to you." I was almost surprised to find my voice worked.

If I felt as if I wasn't enough and should give up, there would be others in the group wrestling with their inner demons, and I knew that none of them had faced anything like this before.

"We can do this," Griffin called back. "If our ancestors fought this evil creature and drove him into the ground, then we can push ourselves to keep going and hold him there. Their blood is in us."

I grinned at the elder's words. He'd given me encouragement and support several times before, but his words had a grit now, as if he knew this was something he could do and that this time it really mattered. I couldn't help but like the gentle elder even more. It turned out his gentleness was built on a strength of character that was going to help them all.

The elder continued to speak out, and conversation happened here and there—stories of overcoming, what mattered to them, why they wanted to see this through, and the positivity of the group lifting. I was able to focus on the magic, listening and appreciating how well everyone was trying to work together.

Just wait. You're all fresh now. But you've got a long way to go, Princess. And you're all going to get very tired.

I gritted my teeth and tried to push the presence from my mind mentally, imagining having it all to myself. I had no way of knowing if it was working or not, but he didn't say anything else so I took it to be a possible positive sign.

His toxic words had planted a seed, however. He had a point, and whether I wanted to admit it or not, everyone struggled the more tired they got. Not thinking, I glanced back toward the edge of the decayed area. It was far enough away from us that it would be difficult for us to get back to the other side of it if we were low on magic.

And we still had a long way to go to get to the center of the area and the gate itself.

I couldn't voice my doubts. I had to lead this group and that meant leading by example. I wasn't going to give up when they needed me to be strong and keep going.

On we trudged, green springing up before us to be a carpet for our feet. The smell of sulfur and noxious gases slowly increased until I was worried about the purity of the air around us, but Flick used some fancy tricks with electricity to create an area of air that seemed to repel the stench. I wasn't sure how he did it, and I was concerned that it drained more energy from one of us, but it brought a little more life back to the group.

After about half an hour, the group fell quiet again amid a general air of discomfort. The sun was higher in the sky now, beating down on us mercilessly. What had been a good day for walking in the woods under the cover of trees was becoming a hot late morning.

On top of that, the heat made the decay worse, and some of the fumes and toxic liquids here and there reflected a swirl of colors that made the eyes swim. It was a hellscape all of its own.

"I think I see something different ahead," Neritas said, his head held higher than mine.

I had gone back to focusing on each step and pushing myself forward bit by bit, but I raised my head to see if I could spot the difference.

At first, I didn't see what what he had seen, but eventually I spotted it too. A differently colored area lay not too far ahead. It wasn't much higher than the ground and I couldn't see anything remarkable about it, but it must have once been something more.

I dared to reach with my mind and felt more than the dark presence that was normally there. I felt magic. Dragon magic, similar to the sword and shield I carried, and if I were closer, I thought I could connect to it.

Having something to focus on helped the group pick up speed a little, and we hurried toward it. It still took several minutes for it to get large enough to see that it was a stone area, paved with large slabs. It had several broken pillars dotted around it, and some that looked as if they were mostly intact.

They were a similar color to the black of the decay around, darkened either over time or perhaps they'd always been that way, and they blended with their surroundings. When we were closer, I noticed a large circle in the center of it—another darker material that could only be the gate.

"We've found it." A strange quality to my voice took even me by surprise. Something about this place created anger within me. Anger that it needed to exist and anger that no one was properly guarding it or maintaining it. How had something so important been left to become so neglected?

With a direction and the stone close enough that we could see it growing wider with each minute, we pushed ahead with more ease until Neritas took the first step onto the stone. He tested the firmness of it for a second before putting all his weight onto it.

"It's solid and won't do us any harm as far as I can tell," he reported.

"It should be safe," Alitas confirmed.

With his wisdom giving me confidence, I stepped up next and moved enough that everyone else would be able to get up and off the decaying land we were fighting.

I hadn't expected to find something so intact in the middle of the decay, and it was a welcome reprieve from using magic. I took one look at the dragons with me and knew that they'd needed it. We'd never have made it back alive had we not been able to stop and recharge now.

CHAPTER FIFTEEN

It was a strange place to rest, right beside the gate to a demonic prison, but something about this area was different from the decaying land. I felt magic emanating from several sources, and it made this small stone circle feel better and less depressive than the land around.

We'd all flopped down as soon as we were safe, and passed around the last of the food and water we'd brought with us. Thankfully Alitas and the guards with him all wore packs full of supplies, enough to go around. He took one look at me and assured me that I didn't need to worry, because we'd still have some left for emergencies.

Crossing the decayed area had sapped us of our strength, but after half an hour of sitting, eating, and looking around at our island in the middle of the rot, we started to recover.

From the center, I could see the tree line in every direction, but I still lamented how far away it was versus how much closer it must have once been. I didn't know how long this place had been left without proper care. Somehow, I had to find a way to heal the land.

Eventually I felt as if I had the strength to stand again. My curiosity about the gate itself and the magic I felt coming from various different spots around the camp got me back to my feet. Griffin stood with me, as did Alitas, Flick, Neritas, Ben and Jace.

It almost made me laugh at the group surrounding me. A mix of those who needed the information and those who wanted to protect me. I didn't think I'd ever get used to being surrounded by people who were there with the sole purpose of keeping me safe and unharmed.

Given how I'd grown up, I was grateful they hadn't been there until recently. My parents had shown some sense in the life they'd given me, even if it had been hard on me. The things I had learned about myself and about what it meant to be alive and a good person, I might never have understood at this age if I'd been a pampered princess my whole life.

Of course, there were times I'd have chosen the royal life. But nothing about my past could be changed, and I couldn't change what had happened here either. All I could do was work out how to go forward and fix as much as possible.

Several points around the circle held magic, all but a couple of pillars emanating some. It felt like some were weaker than others, and I went to these first to see if I could understand why.

"Do these pillars hold magic?" Alitas asked. "Your father always went to check on them one by one, but they've decayed in their own way as well, time wearing them down in much the same way this area has rotted and become a decayed bog that eats anything it touches."

"Yes, they must be part of the protection. Some feel stronger than others and I think at least two are entirely broken." I saw no point in sugarcoating it. We could all see this whole area needed fixing.

"Are they what ought to be charged?" Griffin asked.

"Yes, and if they work like the sword and shield I carry, then only a red dragon can do it."

"Any red dragon?" a guard from the city asked. He had approached us when I wasn't looking.

"Maybe. Both I and my mother can do it, but I've heard that it takes a strong red dragon of the royal line. How true that is I cannot say." It was the most honest answer I could give, and it seemed to satisfy him and his questions.

As I inspected the closest pillar, I found a strange piece of metal in it where the stonework had broken away and exposed it. Somehow, I knew that it was what was holding the magic charge. It had a giant crack down it where the pillar had warped and decayed, and the metal had begun to bend and break as well.

Hoping to confirm what I suspected, I pointed it out to the others and hurried to the nearest pillar that didn't give off any magic signature. It was broken and weathered so badly that I couldn't figure out where to start at first, but I reached out to what looked like a loose bit of rock near the middle and tried to wiggle it.

The stone broke in my hands and revealed what I feared. The metal that ran through the center of the pillar underneath was not only broken into pieces, but it was rusting and looked as if it had been attacked by whatever had rotted the entire area.

Reaching inside the hole, I carefully tried to pull a piece off. It didn't budge, but Alitas pulled out a pocketknife and handed it over.

"Use this to work it free," he suggested.

It didn't take long. His blade was sharp and the piece was easy to loosen once I'd scraped some of the rust away. Ben held an open handkerchief in his palm, and I placed the piece inside.

"Looks like we've got two pillars, at least, to replace with whatever this is, and then a bunch more to repair and maintain," I said.

"And then we'll need you to charge them all up again?" Griffin's face was solemn.

"We'll probably need me and a lot of the dragon community, if not all of it," I replied. "Assuming I can work out how to do it."

"Could you try now?" Jace asked as she took a few photos of what we were seeing. Griffin followed suit and I took a minute to think. Going back to the weaker pillar, I connected to the magic inside it and the connections I had with the group, but when I tried to charge it like the weapon I carried, it shook and gave a high-pitched whine.

I stopped and frowned. Something about that didn't seem right. I went over to one of the most intact pillars and connected to it. It was a lot easier to connect with and seemed to drink in the energy from me. The transference was effortless.

Not wanting to draw too much energy from my companions when we were all still tired and had to journey back, I stopped as soon as I was sure it was working.

"The unbroken and undamaged pillars can be charged by us just fine," I said loud enough for everyone to hear. "And they seem to be hungry."

"Do you think that's what is meant by charging the gate?" Flick moved to the edge of the circle that housed the giant object.

Looking his way, I took in the large door properly for the first time. It had to be fifty yards across and was made of a dark metal that shone despite the way it had aged. In the center of it was something else I could feel. It was a rune of sorts, and the lines depicting it were made of what appeared to be more of the strange metal contained in the pillars.

"No." I moved to stand beside Flick. "The gate has its own charge. I imagine the pillars keep the area safe so we can approach and charge the gate. If we fix the pillars first, we should be able to then charge the gate."

A silence so complete I was startled by it followed my words. It wasn't good news and it made it clear that we had a lot of work before us to sort this out. On the positive side of things, I was sure that everyone here believed the story I'd told and understood the importance of returning and doing what we could to reverse the destruction.

No one here could doubt that the gate needed maintenance. Which left one big question: how long did we have if two pillars had failed already? I estimated that another three weren't functional and that the remaining nineteen were weak and needed a good charge themselves.

You can't hold me in here. You know that, right,

Princess? There aren't enough dragons left and I have done too much damage. It's only a matter of time before I'm free.

We'll see about that, I thought, hoping he could hear me as well as I heard him.

I didn't get a response, so I had no way to know, but I pushed it from my mind. I hadn't come here to argue with an entity I couldn't see. There was more to focus on now that I had more answers and information.

Once everyone had seen the metal and taken photos, Ben folded the handkerchief over it and tucked it deep into a pocket. I was grateful he was taking care of it. I didn't want that responsibility myself and wasn't prepared to trust anyone else with it. I was the sort of person who would invariably lose it or forget about it and have to search everywhere for the location I had decided was a good safe place to keep it in.

To ascertain the state of the other pillars, I went around them all, connecting to see if they would take energy from me and the group. I didn't give them much, but I gave them enough to know that only seventeen were working perfectly. Another two looked to be intact, held charge, and appeared to be doing their job, but they weren't accepting any energy.

With the three different problems to deal with and as many photos as I thought would help, I knew we had done all we could on this visit. It was time to head back.

Having something else to focus on, discover, and learn had brought everyone out of the funk the journey had caused. Several hours had gone by as we'd gathered information from the gate and its platform and protective area. This knowledge was probably in a vault or library somewhere in Detaris, but likely not up to date or in pictures, and nothing that detailed how the magic worked.

At least, nothing that Ben had found so far.

"Is everyone ready to return?" This would be the hard part.

While we had recovered as best we could, it hadn't been long enough or restful enough for us to be entirely recharged and able to use our magic again. But we couldn't stay out here with no shade and no relief as the day got hotter. We also only had so much food and water left to get us back to the cars.

On top of that, a demon lay beneath our feet, and he had more than enough minions around us that they could approach at any moment and make our lives much more difficult. I didn't allow my thoughts to drift to the question of when the worst time for them would be to attack. I wasn't giving this demon any ideas, since he was likely getting at least some inkling of my thoughts.

The group fell back into the same two-person-wide column with me and Neritas at the front and my mother and Delphin at the back. They all looked happy to be heading back the way we'd come, and I hoped that it would be enough to keep us going and stave off the despair this time.

I waited for our green dragons to start healing the land and then we set off. The first few steps were the hardest. The horizon seemed so far away, but I lowered my gaze a little and focused on making the magic part work, using our combined magic to help the green dragons clear and heal a path for us, as well as funneling power from those who couldn't help to those who could.

Unlike on previous occasions where I had been pulling magic from people, I didn't like the feel of it this time. Possibly because I was using it all for a magic skill that didn't come naturally, or because several of the dragons were resisting it a bit.

Still, we made progress, and despite my fears the tree line came closer, and with it a general sense of hopefulness. It was not easy to keep going, and we were slower on the way back. But we knew what we were aiming for, and the oppressive feeling grew fainter with the distance we put between us and the gate.

We were about halfway back when gaps appeared in the group as some of the dragons grew tired. We had no choice but to slow a little, and I stopped pulling magic from them all for a minute or two with the intention of letting them recover a bit. Of course, that added a little extra strain on the rest, but I knew I could also draw on myself a bit more.

Reaching for the sword at my belt, I connected to the energy in it and gently started pulling it out to help replace the energy from the dragons I was giving a break.

It took a few minutes for the group to come back together and start working as a cohesive unit again, but it wasn't long before Neritas stumbled. I caught him to stop him from falling headfirst into the rotten gunk before us.

"Thanks," he said as we paused. We were over halfway back, but still far enough away that any major problems were going to haunt us and make it dangerous.

"Can you keep going?" I tried to keep the fear out of my voice.

"I don't think I want to stop here. Do you?"

"It's not exactly the best of locations to build a house. I

don't think much of the view." I grinned, but I saw the tiredness in his eyes and although he tried to smile back, it was halfhearted.

Instead of making further banter, he carried on, but I noticed that the ground beneath us was barely green and alive before we were putting our feet on it. All around the group, the patch of ground that we were controlling and trying to keep safe was shrinking, and everyone was naturally crowding in a little closer.

In some ways it made things easier for us. Our magic wasn't draining as fast and the dragons were able to work together more easily. But in other ways it made it harder, as we were almost jostling each other and had to walk slower to not trip anyone up. And slower meant we were going to be out here longer, trying to maintain this level of magic.

I drew more heavily on the magic already stored in the weapon and shield I carried, hoping I wouldn't come to regret it later. But if I didn't use it now, we would all die.

The magic flowed out from me and into everyone who needed it, especially the green dragons, boosting their strength and helping us pick up the pace again. Despite the help from me, the green dragons kept our area small, almost as if there had been an unspoken agreement that this was going to be done as efficiently as possible.

Slowly the safe zone came closer and closer until it was a few hundred yards away and I could see guards waiting for us. I fixed my eyes on them, wondering how far away I could connect to them and potentially use their magic. For now, it was still too far.

"We're almost there," I called, hoping it would help

them all dig a little deeper. "Let's all help each other to the finish line."

I didn't know if it would help anyone or not, but I was determined to set a good example. I linked arms with Neritas, giving him support if he needed it. He leaned in my direction, and I felt his exhaustion even more. There wasn't a lot left in him and he knew it.

With only one way to help, I continued to monitor the magic, pulling it from those who weren't green as gently and slowly as I dared, taking as much as I could from the sword and shield and knowing that at least they could handle it.

At the same time, I felt the shadow catchers move.

"I want you all to remain as calm as possible," I said, trying to do the same. "But we really need to walk faster."

Just as I'd feared, right when we were most vulnerable, the demons were coming.

CHAPTER SIXTEEN

No one spoke as the train of dragons I was leading continued to try to make it out of the rotten area influenced by the gate. Because I had been trying to connect to the dragons ahead of us, I had stretched out my mind and had as much notice as possible that the demons were on the move and all heading toward us.

That warning was about all I could be thankful for in that moment.

We were in a lot of danger and the dragons I was with didn't need me to keep pointing it out. They all knew we needed to hurry.

On top of that, I had become aware of several aches and pains. My body was still recovering from the beating I had taken, and the day's activities were taking a toll despite the healing I'd received. Somehow I had to ignore it and carry on, however. They needed me to.

We still had about three hundred yards to go when the group started to divide. An area of rotting grass formed between the two sections as the green dragons waned and struggled to keep going at the same pace.

The second group panicked, none of them moving as one of the green dragon guards Alitas had commanded to help us almost fainted.

"Get this group to the edge," I said to Neritas, pulling away from the front of the group to let it pass and get back to the dragons in trouble.

I kept connected to their magic as I fought to make my own safe patch and stand out of their way and then get back to the others. Although I'd drawn a little on my own magic so far, I had kept my magic ticking along better than some of the others, aware that this whole plan would fall apart if I passed out.

Now I threw caution to the wind and poured out the magic from myself, pumping it into the green dragons behind to stabilize the group and give Neritas a little bit of a boost so he could lead his group alone.

My guard and constant friend didn't let me down. He lifted his voice and encouraged the eight dragons who had managed to stay with him, including Jace, to get back to the safe zone and stick close.

I rejoined the other dragons as soon as I could, seeing the exhausted look on my mother's face as she tried to do what I had been doing for the front of the group.

With me taking over and the extra energy I could give them, the rotten patches started to become healthy green grass and moss again. It took a few seconds for them to form up again, but I slipped into the group, a few rows back, right behind Griffin, knowing that of all of them, he was the dragon I needed to get home safe the most.

Onward we trudged as the chaos in my mind grew. The shadow catchers were so close that we saw the first few as they came out of the tree line to the north and south of us and started to make a beeline right for us. Neritas and his group were about a hundred yards away from the trees by then, but we were easily twice that.

"It's all right," I said as soon as panic made the dragons with me slow again. "We can get out of this, but I need you all to focus. I can fight and kill them, but I don't want to do it out here. Let me get you safe and then I can do what I do best and slay some demons."

The confidence in my voice earned me a few looks of surprise from those who had never seen me fight the creatures, but all of them calmed again.

"All gate guard dragons will go into defense mode the moment they're in the safe zone to protect the other dragons," Alitas called loudly enough that both groups could hear him.

I smiled at the novelty and badassery of having someone so in command as part of my group. This dragon had trained for this, and he was on my side.

"All right, we're not far behind," I said to my group, aware I was draining fast as I stretched my connection to Neritas and continued to help the first group get safe. "Keep it up and we'll be sorted in no time."

Although I wanted to look to the sides to see how fast the shadow catchers were coming toward us, I didn't need to. I felt them rushing straight for me and my vulnerable group. At this rate, we were going to need a miracle.

I wasn't about to give up, however. There had been more than one occasion when I had looked at the danger and had no idea how I might survive it, yet here I was, standing in the middle of a field of decay that should have been killing me, surrounded by dragons I was keeping alive. I always had hope and the knowledge that I wasn't alone.

My group was still traveling slower than Neritas, despite the energy I was feeding them, and the connection I had to them was soon cut. The distance was too great. It took away some of what was taxing me, but it also took away their support when they still had twenty yards to go.

Alitas roared in defiance and urged them all on. His words were lost to me but his manner was not. They almost all ran the last of the gap, not waiting for the green dragons to fully heal the land for them.

"That's it. Look, the first group has made it and we're not far behind," I promised as I helped the group I had even more.

Trying not to panic them at the predicament we were in and how certain I was that the shadow catchers would reach us before we got to the tree line, I simply hoped and fought on. I saw five demons, although two were lagging behind. More were in the trees ahead, traveling slower but still coming toward us.

It was going to be hard to fend off that many and punch a gap through somewhere to get everyone back to the cars, but I reminded myself that Alitas had a backup plan. I wasn't out of escape routes either.

That didn't stop my heart racing and my palms from growing sweaty. I also felt tired. My magic was fueling my group so much that I was running out as well. The sword and shield were almost entirely drained when we were still over a hundred yards away, and I couldn't draw on them either.

I tried to see if I could connect to the fresher dragons up ahead of us. One of them was just about in reach, standing right near the edge.

Hoping he didn't mind, I connected and pulled from his magic, making sure I was looking directly at him when I did. He seemed to step back with a start, but then he looked up and caught my gaze. Even from this far away, he looked taken aback or scared by what I was doing, but I kept it as gentle as I could, taking the bare minimum to help the green dragons I was with.

It kept me from passing out as we hurried along. Each ten yards felt like a mile as the shadow catchers came closer and closer. I reached for more and more connections as I saw more and more guards gather, Alitas calling what seemed like a small army to him. As I could draw on more of them and not feel so guilty, I fueled Neritas again, hoping he would feel it and come back to help.

When the demons were almost upon us, two more guards stepped forward with Neritas to create a path out toward us again.

"Run for safety," I commanded all of them as soon as I was sure they'd make it. The green dragons with me gritted their teeth and put one last amount of effort into making a causeway.

Some of them squealed as the first demon got to us and tried to stab one of the city guards. I hurried toward it, not caring if I had rot underneath my feet, charging my boots in case the green dragons couldn't help me yet. I charged the sword and shield as I sprinted. Within a second I was crashing into the demon with the shield and stabbing it in the side.

It let out a barbaric screech as the ground under my feet turned green and solidified some. Grinning like a maniac, I hit it again with both sword and shield, battering with one and slashing with the other.

Within a few more seconds the demon died, turning into a strange puff of smoke. The air was still, with no breeze despite the openness of the area, and it hung there as I turned and looked for the next demon. It was a couple of yards away, and my mother and Reijo were standing against it so the back of the group was still protected.

I ran at it from behind and finished it off for her. As it also became a smoke cloud, I ran through it, shuddering at the chill it put up my spine and not daring to breathe until I was on the other side of it. Mom gave me a determined nod and the three of us sprinted the last section to the tree line where everyone else was now safe and Alitas had them in a group surrounded by his guards.

The next demon came at me as we were reaching safety, forcing me to stop a little way from the edge and fight some more. Neritas stepped forward with me this time, using his shield to help push it back as well.

Mom joined me on the other side, and we worked as a team, pushing the shadow catcher back and hurting it where we could. Several times it lashed out with its vicious beak but each time, it clanged against a shield, hurting itself as much as jarring the arm that blocked it.

With every opening, I tried to attack as well, sometimes missing and sometimes cutting at the shadow that made up the strange body. I had gotten used to the way the damage showed now and trusted that if I hit it with something, I was making progress and hurting it until it became nothing but vapor, and I fought automatically.

More kept coming, however, forcing us to fall back and others in the group to keep fighting them off on other sides.

More came into the area my mind could feel as well, the unease growing despite how many we fought off.

"We need to get out of here or we're going to get pinned down until I can't fight any longer," I told Alitas when I found the honor guard close to me. I wasn't sure if he heard me at first, as he was focused on fending off another shadow catcher and keeping the dragons near him safe. He managed to push it back as I charged the shield in his hand, and Flick stabbed it with a spear I'd charged for him.

It pushed the creature back and allowed me to step in and take over the fight, drawing the monster's attention as Alitas moved toward the group.

"Everyone, follow me," he called before heading toward a small path that looked overgrown.

At first the group hesitated, but the nearest guards to him ushered the more scared and less capable dragons off after him. Griffin was one of the first to go. The guards interspersed themselves, with Jace, Harriet, Tim, and Cios also spreading themselves out. I encouraged my mom to go with Reijo toward the middle of the group.

With how tired she was feeling, it was better that she was safe.

I was left with the usual group of mixed color dragons, a guard I didn't know taking the place of Capricia. A lot of us were low on magic, but we had become so efficient at fighting and my abilities were so much better that we killed another two shadow catchers before we ran after the others.

I felt shadow catchers still in the area, but a lot of them were heading to a part of the path behind me, their directions from whoever controlled them outdated. There were only a few demons out in front. On top of that, I had seen Alitas and his companions fight well and I had some faith that if any demons got to the group, they could keep everyone safe until I or my mother could help kill them.

Not having to fight alone and being able to trust the dragons around me made a huge difference to the fight, and I felt more optimistic again. I didn't doubt that heading away from the gate was also helping with that. The largest oppressive force on my mind and the biggest source of unease was growing less prominent. On top of that, between us, we had dispatched several shadow catchers, and not all of the kill strikes had been mine.

Everyone was growing weary now, however, and running along a small path, pushing past bushes, sometimes ducking under trees and around other obstacles was taking yet another physical toll.

I was in a lot of pain, but it was something I could live with for now. The healing device would have to repair whatever was still not okay when we finally got safe. I couldn't let the misguided attack from the dragons in Detaris put this mission and all the dragons with me at risk. I had to push through.

"Almost there," I heard Alitas call from somewhere up ahead.

It gave me extra strength and I helped encourage those

in front of me, ushering them on ahead. I had no idea where we were going, but I suspected from the state of the path and the fact that he was the only one who knew the way that this was the alternative exit he had spoken of.

With no knowledge of where it led, I wasn't sure what to do about Capricia sitting in a car in the parking lot, or the belongings we all had in those vehicles and would need to get back to at some point soon.

Because I couldn't trust anyone else with what mattered to me most, I'd stashed it all in the pack on my back, but that made it heavier than I'd have liked—clearly not the wisest decision I had made of late, but at least I wasn't worried about my own personal items.

Before we reached our destination, another shadow catcher caught up with us, coming in from our left side. Delphin held it off, blocking and stabbing at it with his walking stick until I could get to his side with Neritas and help. Flick also joined in, the pair of them still making it their goal to keep me as safe as they could.

I appreciated it, as the four of us quickly surrounded the creature and attacked it from all sides. Delphin and I blocked the attacks and kept it from hurting any dragons running to safety.

Although it didn't take long to kill it as a team, everyone else was ahead down the path before we were done and could follow. At first, I was anxious about being left behind, unable to see anyone, but Delphin took the lead as if he also knew where he was going.

Thankfully we caught up with the group quickly. Alitas was already waving everyone down some stone steps into a hole in the ground. It was overgrown, and a stone slab beside it looked as if it had been pulled away.

Several of the group must have already been inside, and my mom was a short way in making herself glow slightly.

I ushered everyone else vulnerable inside as I joined the defensive group outside and fought off another couple of shadow catchers. The second one almost took us by surprise, getting a glancing hit on Delphin before Neritas blocked the attack with his shield.

While Delphin pulled back in pain, I moved in to cover his position and brought my shield up to defend him. I wobbled immediately, dizzy and exhausted. We were all almost completely drained of magic, and all I dared use now was the little stored in the sword and shield as I fought the demon in front of me.

Tired and more cautious, it took me longer than I'd have liked to kill the demon. By the time I was done, I was painfully aware of how much magic I had used. My whole body ached.

Both sword and shield were out of energy, and everyone around me was panting hard.

"Inside, quickly. Before more arrive. We can't fight another."

I watched them all hurry away, not wanting to go before any of them, until Alitas and I were the only ones standing outside.

"Go," he instructed me. "I need to pull this slab over after us."

"I will help from inside." I didn't intend to leave him either.

If he thought about arguing, he had enough sense to not

to do so while in action, and we both hurried down the steps and into the area underneath. It smelled slightly damp, but it also had a warm earthy scent that made it seem inviting. It was wholesome after the rot of the area around the gate.

Alitas stopped and grabbed the slab edge, and I did the same, helping him slide it across while my mind focused on giving him aid from the last traces of magic left inside us to help him feel strong enough.

We had precious few seconds before the shadow catchers could get close enough to see us. Not that they always needed to see. They were capable of following scents and sounds, but I hoped that we could at least make a start at getting away from them now.

As I made myself glow, Alitas fished in his pack for an old-fashioned flashlight, and between us we illuminated the beginning of a long corridor under the earth. Stone pillars and a slabbed ceiling and floor kept the tunnel sound.

It went south and a little east, but most importantly, it went away from the gate and danger.

CHAPTER SEVENTEEN

I joined the others in heading through the tunnel, excited about seeing where it led.

Alitas didn't know. He had simply been told that it was a backup option should one be needed. As such, he insisted on going first, and I followed close behind. If we were leading everyone into danger, I wanted to be able to react first.

Now that we were all together as a group, we were moving at a gentle but steady pace, making sure everyone was okay. We'd passed around a little more food and water but were now low on both.

Thankfully being underground was a cool relief after a morning in the scorching heat. I didn't doubt that many of us were burned from so much time in the sun.

After having taken stock of all the flashlights, batteries, and phones that could be used to light the way, and knowing there were two red dragons as backup to light the way, we had some kind of light glowing every three people and everyone was resting and recharging their magic again.

I'd drained everyone with me far more than I'd normally want to, but I had kept us all alive, and with Delphin sporting the only injury, it had been worth it. Of course, if we got out of this whole situation alive, we would be happy with what we'd learned and how we had succeeded.

Despite the tunnel sloping down for a while and being a significant distance beneath the surface, I continued to keep my mind open to the feel of the demonic in the area so I'd know if one found the tunnels we were in and came rushing after us. It wasn't perfect and foolproof as a method, as my mind was not attuned to sensing what was nearby and how far it was from me.

Now and then I picked up on a shadow catcher that felt close and knew we were traveling through the tunnel only a few yards to one side of it but far enough down that it wouldn't have any idea we had passed so close by. With us gone from the surface and the entrance unknown to the creatures, they appeared to have fallen into a sentry mode, guarding the gate area.

I was grateful for now. It allowed me to focus more on where we were. We'd traveled through the tunnel at least a few miles, and it showed no sign of ending. A couple of times, we had come across sections where a wall had begun to shift and slide inward, but so far everything had been intact enough to navigate.

It made me wonder how long this tunnel had been here, and who had built it and why. Had one of my ancestors understood the need to be careful and put this in place for the future? Did someone know that one day the gate might be neglected and someone would have to come here without the protection of the entire force needed to keep the area safe?

I had no one left to ask. My mother had been as surprised as I was to know the tunnel existed and had no idea where it would lead either.

The tunnel seemed to go straight, but these sorts of things could easily turn gradually over a long distance and put the person using them out by a long way when they emerged on the other end. At first the gate had continued to goad me, the presence in my mind still foreboding, but we'd got too far away for me to easily sense it now.

Feeling tired from the march on top of everything and aware that our group had spread out a little more as others slowed and struggled to match the pace, I paused to catch my breath. Alitas responded immediately and came to my side.

"Any idea how much further?" I asked, but he shook his head and continued to hold his flashlight where it could show us the most detail forward.

The tunnel simply kept going.

"Do you feel much more evil out here?" he asked.

As he spoke I realized he had made a good point and that I couldn't feel any real danger anymore. We were safer than we had been all day.

After a fifteen-minute rest, I encouraged everyone to start moving again. Griffin worked his way forward as we did so.

"I want to say thank you," he said once he was walking along near me. The tunnel was too narrow to have two abreast. I moved a little to one side and let him come close enough to be easily heard and share the light Alitas held with us.

"Seeing you, your friends and your mother in action fighting those things, as well as everything you did to keep us safe while traveling to and from the gate… It was very selfless of you, and I know it must have cost you a lot."

"It's what's needed and something only I can do. I've always thought that the point of life is to find the unique that only we can be and to do our best at being it." I smiled at him, grateful for the encouragement and appreciation. I hoped it was something he could carry to the other elders of the city and then the people.

I might not be perfect, but I could help the dragon world and I just wanted to play the role that only I could.

Griffin fell silent after this, and I tried to think of something to say. I wanted to ask him if he thought there was any chance the city would accept me now. I didn't dare, no matter how tempting it was.

Thankfully the silence that formed between us didn't last long or have time to get awkward. Alitas illuminated what looked like a room of some kind ahead and gave me hope that we had reached the end of the tunnel.

We hurried forward, letting everyone behind know a wider space was ahead of us. As we got closer, it looked more and more like an exit. Steps went up to the left of the room, and interestingly, another tunnel led away from the other side. It wasn't lined with stone in the same way, though, and it looked worryingly unstable to anyone who was trying to go farther.

I stopped Alitas from going too far up the steps until we

had everyone gathered in the room and accounted for. They all looked more tired than I'd ever seen them, and I had no way of knowing what more we would have to do to get back to safety, but I was also proud of them. A sit down in the evening sun might do them all some good.

While they were gathering and several guards were in conversation with Alitas, figuring out how to get out, I closed my eyes and focused my abilities. When we'd first arrived in this area there had been a lot of shadow catchers on the edge of my mind, all of them following but not attacking. And when they had made a move, it had almost been overwhelming.

If we were going to emerge from this tunnel, I wanted some idea of what we faced before we did so. That way we could prepare for the worst and hope for the best.

A few seconds later I picked up on a faint sense of unease off to the northwest, but nothing that would make me want to run. Although I hadn't used the magic directly and calmly like this much, it felt as if I was learning to extend my reach still and these shadow catchers were the sort of creatures that often lingered just out of my senses. To feel them out there now was helpful and a sign that I was growing.

I'd suspected some lingered nearby many times, but this felt like confirmation of it. I could sense them. But could they sense me? I had no way to know, but it was an indication that they might have been able to. I liked that theory more than the possibility that someone close to me was betraying me again and again, especially when we'd worked out that it could only be Ben.

As I felt outwards, I thought I sensed something

else, off to one side of the room we were in—a dull feeling of magic, but it was faint and I couldn't place exactly where it was. There wasn't a tunnel in that direction as far as I could see, but now wasn't the time to find out.

When we were all together and everyone had five minutes to prepare mentally and generally, I gave Alitas the nod and moved closer, in case we'd come face-to-face with a danger I couldn't sense.

It looked as if another stone slab needed to be lifted and slid out of the way of the entrance. Several of the more buff men moved to help him push it up, and although I considered joining in, I wasn't the strongest physically and I needed to save my strength. I stayed close, though, ready to help in other ways.

They appeared to struggle in vain. The slab moved a little and dirt rained down. I frowned and again considered helping, but they only paused a moment to get their breath before Alitas had them brace the slab and count into another push. Most of the lights in the room were shining on the group, showing what was going on and letting us see what they were up against.

This time the slab shifted more, and dirt slipped down in larger amounts and the odd small root appeared. They had to stop and set it down again—all of them were already panting and looking at each other as if they weren't sure this was going to work.

As they paused, longer this time, I considered how much dirt and debris might have built up on top of the slab with years and years of the exit being unknown and not maintained. It was possible we couldn't get out this way.

And that would give us only one option. To go back the way we'd come.

I didn't like the thought of it, especially given how little food and drink we had left. If we had to go back, we would have a group of exhausted, hungry, and dehydrated dragons, some of whom were old and frail. And we'd have an army of shadow catchers to fight through again.

Starting to fear that we would have no choice, I went to help, slipping into a gap. Some of the others stepped up as well, until we had as many people under the slab as would fit. Not everyone was the strongest, but at this point every little bit of effort could make a difference.

With another countdown from Alitas, we pushed again. Everyone strained hard as more dirt shifted. Near the top of the stairs, the dragons could get more lift, pushing up from their legs and having a natural advantage. That edge gave, and dirt slid down the stairs in a small avalanche that almost knocked several of them off their feet.

Daylight came through, making everyone cheer. More dragons helped us, coming to clear some of the dirt away, using their hands to widen the gap we'd created. As soon as she could, Jace squeezed through the gap and, once on top, used a shield like a spade to dig some of the dirt away. I squeezed through to do the same and help shift the slab from outside.

More and more dragons came through as we made the opening safer and wider, until we were finally all on the outside of the tunnels. It was late, the sun was starting to set, and no one was in a hurry to do more than stand or sit. I didn't blame them, and let everyone take a breather while we tried to work out exactly where we were. We were in what must have once been a clearing but was now more overgrown with a few young trees here and there.

The entrance to the tunnels was near the base of a large tree, which had grown over the entrance. I felt bad that we had disturbed so many of its roots, but the green dragons stepped forward and repaired the damage, growing the new roots out and around the tunnel door, almost framing it and making it look like a magical doorway into the beyond.

"I don't think we're far from the cars," Jace reported, looking at the maps on her phone. "We've swung down south of them and we're on the other side of the road. It shouldn't be too difficult to find a route back as long as we're careful with the wildlife and can find a path through these trees."

"We can make a path if nature is all that's in our way," Delphin pointed out as the group of green dragons smiled.

I was amused by their bravado, but I understood that was all it was right now. They were all exhausted and needed to rest as well. This had been harder on them of all of us.

The rest of our supplies were in the cars, and the longer we stayed in one place, the more likely we were to attract demons to us. I didn't let the group rest for too long.

"Will we be able to find this place again if we leave it as it is?" I asked Alitas. "I would like to return and see what else is down there another time."

"I will get you back here one way or another if it is your wish." His face showed me sincere confidence.

I blinked a few times, not sure how to respond to such a sentiment. This dragon was far older, more experienced, and stronger than I was, and here he was, telling me that anything I wanted, he'd give his full skills and talents to make it happen. I wasn't used to that after feeling as if I had to prove I was worthy all the time to the elders in Detaris.

We moved out as a group, heading back toward the cars and trekking through the forest. It was easier than we'd hoped. A path appeared about fifty feet from where we were, going in almost the exact direction we wished to go. Time had also made it smaller and more overgrown, as if the forest was reclaiming it the way it had at the other end of the path.

An hour later, we were walking into the small dirt parking lot, a larger and wiser, but dirtier and more tired group than when we had left that morning.

"There's a car missing," Jace said immediately, pointing out what I had also noticed right away. The car Capricia had been driving was gone, and so was she.

"I guess she returned to the city." I frowned, not keeping the anger from my voice.

"She did." A gate guard stepped out of the forest on the other side as everyone else who had come by car moved toward the ones that were left.

"We'll drive you wherever you need to go," Alitas offered. The guards that he commanded gathered to him, now that they felt their task was done.

"I'm taking my group back to the boat to rest in safety," Jace told me. "You're all welcome to join us until I can get another car or two to take everyone back to the city to present all the new evidence to the elders."

It was a well-timed offer from her, and Griffin—one of

the dragons who had effectively been abandoned—expressed gratitude.

"To the boat it is," Alitas confirmed. "I'll leave a basic guard here and the rest will also join us and see what you wish of us going forward."

Again, I was shocked by their ready allegiance, but I nodded as if this was perfectly normal and acceptable, partially distracted by Griffin. He was tired, and his shoulders slumped, but finding Capricia gone had resulted in what I could only put down to anger. His jaw was set as he stared at the spot where the car had been.

Although he was trying to be subtle, he'd clenched and unclenched his fists when the guard had confirmed that she'd gone off to the city. He wasn't happy with what she'd done, and I wasn't surprised. Capricia had been commanded to come with us to protect him and make sure he got the evidence needed and returned safely.

Instead, she had abandoned him right when it was about to get dangerous and made it harder on the rest of us by heading back to the city with a good chunk of our supplies and some of the belongings my companions had left in the car. It made me glad everything that mattered to me was still in the pack I carried.

As Alitas had two more cars brought around from the other end of the parking lot and Griffin was offered a ride in the largest, the emotion seemed to fade. I got in with him and sat in the middle at the back. Flick and Neritas got in on either side of me in their usual positions.

When Alitas drove off, I relaxed. For the first time all day, I finally felt safe.

CHAPTER EIGHTEEN

The yacht was a welcome sight, though we had so many dragons now that it would take more than two trips in the smaller motorboats to get everyone out to it.

As we parked on the shore, I noticed cars already there and a single new dragon waiting. Jace went up to him like she knew him and Cios followed. They both hugged this newcomer and Cios gave him a hearty slap on the back.

"Are they safe on the boat already?" Jace asked as I moved closer, wanting to be introduced and hoping for an explanation.

"There's more dragons here?" I asked. I needed to know what was going on.

"Yes. When I fed back what we'd seen and done, they came to talk to you and everyone else here as well." Jace spoke as if this was understandable.

"Forgive me if this seems rude, but I consider it my duty to protect Scarlet now. Who is waiting for her, and are they perfectly safe?" Alitas directed his question at Jace, and for a second I thought she might smack him in response. The brash woman was not the kind to like being questioned, no matter how politely. Instead of being irritated, she broke into a broad grin.

"You can keep your sword in its sheath, Alitas. It's Elias and Sarai. I'm pretty sure you remember them, right?"

He smiled and nodded.

"Yes. It would be good to see them again."

"Elias?" my mother asked. "He's here?"

Once again, I raised my eyebrows and looked between them all. It seemed this group of dragons had all heard of each other and knew of deeds that I didn't. Yet another reminder that I had a lot to learn.

I was eager to get over to the yacht, but I was still the line of defense for a lot of these dragons, so I encouraged everyone into the first two boats. Alitas tried to get me to head over, but I refused. I insisted my mother take Griffin and introduce him to the legendary dragons he'd only heard of. All he knew was that they were older than most of us, even him, and important in some way.

While we waited for the boats to return, I looked over who I had left with me. It was mostly the dragons who had insisted on protecting me. As we waited there, another car pulled up, and several more buff dragons got out carrying the shields and spears that all the other gate guards did.

Alitas brought them to where I was standing, on the shore of the lake.

"This is Kryos, my second in command. He also served your father briefly before the end." Alitas indicated a slightly younger dragon wearing a ripped t-shirt revealing bulging muscles. His hair was a shock of purple spiked up in a mohawk . He was older than Neritas at a glance, but not by much, and I caught the two glancing at each other.

Before I could respond in any way, Kryos bowed to me.

"Your Majesty, I vowed to serve your line when I was still a very young dragon. I stand by that vow now. My life is at your disposal."

"Thank you," I replied as he straightened. "I don't know if I'm much of a queen, but I promise to try and be responsible and respectful of the service you offer me and to do my best to protect those around me regardless."

"Then I am already pledging myself to the right person." He grinned and offered to shake hands with everyone around me.

I introduced everyone, making a point of telling all the dragons who had arrived, but especially Alitas, what Neritas and Flick had already done for me. Ben also joined in, telling them how he'd seen Neritas and Flick fly around me protectively on more than one occasion. The beating I had taken was also mentioned, and for a short while I didn't have to hide how much pain I was in as my wounds were discussed and understanding was offered.

"While I am saddened that you were made to feel so unwelcome in any dragon city, it is clear that you have two at your side with the hearts and minds of honor guards. If you have accepted them as such, then I am proud to call them brothers as well." Kryos bowed again before the boats arrived and drew our attention that way.

"Some of us will stay on shore. I don't think the yacht will hold all of us," Alitas said when I suggested some of his guards go with the second wave. "And we will want to be sure no other threats of any kind disturb you while out there."

"But many of you also need rest in safety." I met his gaze. I wasn't going to stand for any argument. "I wouldn't be keeping the promise I've just made if I didn't insist that at least the weariest of you came with me to also benefit from the sanctuary, even if only for a few hours, before you trade places and take shifts and things like that."

Alitas smirked slightly and I got the impression he wasn't used to being talked to in the way I just had.

Although my feet were aching and my head was light, I was determined to see everyone else safe as well. And that meant hanging back for the third and final group to be taken to the yacht. Ben didn't look happy about being asked to go in the second group, but Jace and several of the city guards went with him.

My mother had already gone, and that gave me some comfort that everyone on the yacht was protected by a red dragon as well. Not that they were as likely to need it, but it made some sense. It left a small group of all the colors on the shore.

Alitas wanted to take the first watch around the lake, but Kryos took charge, allowing Alitas to relax a little more while we all sat on the shore and watched the sun set across the water. For a moment the world was beautiful and calm.

At least until my stomach rumbled.

We hadn't eaten a lot that day, as the events had taken a lot longer than planned, but I could wait a little longer. It made everyone else talk about their favorite meals, however.

I tried not to listen to it, as it didn't help me be patient for food, but I appreciated such a normal conversation after being on edge all day.

It wasn't long before we were watching the boats return for the final group. It wasn't going to be a full group, and the previous one hadn't been either, which was a good thing as I wasn't sure the yacht could take more than about twenty-five dragons and I had somehow gathered far more to me than that.

When I thought about how many followers I had acquired whose names I didn't know yet, it struck me as almost crazy. I might not be a queen, but I had a small army already forming.

Not that I thought all of them would stick with me in any battle. The city guards were here because Capricia had chosen them. I got the impression that they didn't particularly want to stay but didn't have the guts to leave either.

Only once I was happy that all the dragons who needed rest were on the boats as well did I get in one. I also used my mind to do one last check of the area, but I couldn't feel any shadow catchers, not even lingering at the very edges of my mind. For now, we seemed to be left in peace. I wasn't sure how long it would last, but it made me feel less guilty for heading away from the dragons left guarding the shore with the sole purpose of trying to keep us safe.

I considered the day's events as we approached the yacht, but those thoughts were pushed from my mind the moment I was onboard and spotted Sarai. The elderly but fierce dragon was sitting on the deck, off to one side with Jace, and the two of them were having an animated conversation in hushed voices.

Already wary of people unhappy with my decisions or who I was, I half expected someone to jump up and tell me that I couldn't be queen and I needed to go back to LA and stop being a disgrace to the dragon race. Instead, my mother appeared with a tray of food for me, and some of the others followed her with drinks.

Gratefully, my companions and I found a place to sit and eat. It didn't take long for Elias and Sarai to realize that I had come aboard and join me.

"Greetings again, Scarlet," Elias said as he came closer and smiled at me, his wrinkled face lighting up. Sarai was less excited and seemed to be here reluctantly. Her attention wandered and her foot tapped.

"Hello, all. I must admit I didn't expect to see either of you so far from your own farmhouse." I tried to smile as if this was a normal situation, but I wasn't sure I managed to win over Sarai.

"We needed to travel, and you were on the way. And Jace has been telling us some amazing things."

I glanced over at the dragon, but she had her back partially turned to tuck into food of her own now that Sarai wasn't grilling her.

"Why don't you both eat with me if you haven't already, and I'll tell you everything that's happened today?"

Before Sarai could object, Elias accepted, and the dragon guards leaped up to sort out a proper table, more food, and generally make my wishes happen—not just for me, but when some of the dragons who worked with Jace helped, I suspected it was also a courtesy for Elias.

Ten minutes later, I was explaining the events we'd been through while eating and recharging. Despite being curious and eager for information, they didn't ask many questions. Elias especially seemed to take it at face value and believe that I was telling him everything and not lying.

Neritas and Flick occasionally dropped into the conversation, telling their version of events or clarifying something I hadn't explained well. It helped. It made me feel like alone I could be good at a bunch of things, but together everything was so much better.

By the time I had finished my story, everyone had eaten, and we were all gathered around with hot drinks. The night was dark outside and the stars shone overhead. Now and then I noticed the gentle rocking of the yacht and felt grateful that we had such a peaceful safe haven so close to the gate. There might be something about Elias and his group of dragons that the city didn't like, but he was good at keeping the dragons with him safe.

"It sounds as if we need to act sooner than we thought," Elias said. "If you all struggled to get to the gate itself and you're some of the most powerful dragons we know, then there is a serious problem."

"It's not as bad as it was," Alitas put in as he looked up from his phone. "I've only just had it confirmed or I'd have said sooner, but the gate's influence has shrunk since this morning. Only by about a foot, but the green dragons on guard duty up there were able to heal the land a little further in."

"A foot is not much of a difference," Sarai pointed out in her usual caustic tone.

I gaped, still trying to take this in. Had we done something to weaken the demon or strengthen the gate just by going there?

"No, it's not," my mother shot back. "But Scarlet added a little power to each of the functioning pillars and the gate itself. Just a little to test which ones were working or not. It must have made a difference. If the right group returned and there were fewer shadow catchers there in general, we could buy ourselves some more time."

My mother's idea was a solid one and it gave me hope that I could make a little progress until we could fully charge the gate. Maybe I didn't need to unite every dragon on the planet. Maybe I just needed enough of the more powerful ones.

"Do I need to remind you all that we almost died today? On more than one occasion." Jace folded her arms across her chest, but rather than confrontational, her voice was sad. "And that was while being able to avoid most of the shadow catchers. If we started to go there regularly with the sole intention of powering the gate, you can bet those shadow catchers will attack us while we're out there on that stone platform."

"Not to mention that we don't know how to fix the two broken pillars yet or power the ones that seem to be damaged. I might have bought us a little more time, but there's no denying we're in serious trouble." It hurt to admit that Jace was right. I wanted to go back to the gate in the morning with all the dragons we had and power it up as much as we dared, but that was a foolish desire.

Ben took this moment as his cue to get the handkerchief out and show everyone the piece of metal we took.

"This is what we need to somehow replicate. Whatever this is that has been set into the pillars." He showed it to all the newcomers who hadn't been there. Elias requested a small piece to take with him, and I approved Ben letting him take some. I expected him to break it in half, but he simply scraped off a small flake that looked as if it had almost rusted off and put it into a pot.

"I think it's the same metal as this sword and shield," I added as I lifted them and made the lines along them glow. "They appear to be able to store magic in some way and then make it easier to use."

"There's probably some component that helps to channel the energy in the right way. A combination of magic and technology. Not all these things are lost to the ages. If I could have a technician dragon and myself take a direct look, then we might be able to work out how to replicate what was needed and repair the damaged pillars. Either way, we're at your service in this matter."

I thanked yet another dragon pledging to help me, but then I yawned, and this seemed to end our little meeting.

"I think we should all get some sleep and figure out the best course of action in the morning. It's been a long day." Ben looked at me with concern in his eyes.

Although I wanted to sleep knowing what I would do the following day, I had a feeling it wasn't going to be an easy discussion and I was going to have to push things in the direction I thought best. Ben had the right idea in suggesting I sleep and rest before then. I would have a better mind, my body would have healed some more, and I'd have more strength to hold my moral compass true and to protect as many as I could.

CHAPTER NINETEEN

Breakfast was once again perfect on the yacht, and I realized I could get used to living on it. After all the time I had been living in the dragon city and in my tiny apartment in LA, I was used to not having masses of space for anything important, and I liked waking up to nature and being able to see the stars at night and the blue of sky and green of nature during the day.

It put me in a good mood despite everything the day would entail. The mood was helped by knowing that we had achieved what we set out to do the day before and had made a difference. It didn't matter that it had been taxing.

Delphin had been almost fully healed by my mother, and she had gone over my wounds as well, although they were already doing much better from having a couple of days of aid from the magical device. Another day or two of rest and they would be completely gone, but I doubted today would be any different from the day before. Busy, full of danger, and a lot of conflict and difficult decision-making.

Despite knowing what was probably coming, I was optimistic. We had a path, of sorts, and I knew that we could power up the gate and its protections again if we had the right mix of dragons, magic, and tech.

I hadn't realized how much it had been weighing on me to feel like I had to unite the entire dragon race to power the gate. I didn't deny that it probably would help if I did—the more power the better—but it wouldn't require every single dragon as far as I could tell. It just needed enough dragons over enough time.

That was an entirely different situation.

Despite this revelation, the dragon city still needed proof, and the elder we'd brought with us needed to return to safety. I had to work out the next best step and the one after that, and I had to do it fast.

I had been tired, but still I had struggled to sleep as my mind went over this exact problem multiple times. I also wanted to go and power the gate up some more, kill more shadow catchers, and get Elias the information he needed as accurately as possible. But that was a dangerous move, and I didn't have enough dragons for that.

Of course, there were more in Detaris. A lot more, but they might not help us. After everything else they had objected to, I worried that they wouldn't want to help us no matter what we told them.

Still, I had to decide. I was soon surrounded by the dragons on the yacht, all of them looking to me for guidance. I scanned the packed deck, seeing encouraging, supportive faces, indifferent expressions, and the suspicion of dragons whose captain had run off and not been seen since. No one was coming from the same place, and no one would react the same way to whatever I said, and I needed to navigate it all.

"What's the plan, Red?" Jace asked when no one else spoke. "We'll see this through until that demon is locked up tight again."

"Thank you. I think we need more dragons, more equipment, and more knowledge, but I don't want to leave it long and I want to be methodical about it. I am, however, encouraged by yesterday that we don't need much more of any of them to have what we need. But when we next go to the gate, I want us to be prepared and at our best. I made a promise to some of you yesterday that I would protect anyone standing with me, and now I want to extend that promise. I want to protect all dragons and all humanity. I want to keep this world safe, but I want to do it in a way that keeps all of you as safe as possible along the way."

When I finished speaking, I noticed I was shaking. I had gotten nervous so gradually that until that moment, I hadn't realized how much I felt it.

"So we're going back to Detaris?" Griffin asked.

"Yes, most of us. Although I want to make a slight detour first. You are welcome to stay here and wait while I do it. I'm hoping that it won't take long."

"Detour where?" Jace spoke with more curiosity than anything else in her voice. "I'm planning on coming with you wherever you go, just so you know."

I felt the corner of my mouth twitch up as I thought about the best explanation to give. This was going to seem a little strange to some of them.

"I want to go back to the place we were yesterday, right at the end. I am pretty sure there was something magical there and I wonder if it might help us or provide further understanding."

"And you want to do that first?" Sarai raised her eyebrows as if this was the stupidest thing she'd heard.

"Yes, but it should be a quick and easy reconnaissance. I just want to see what it is while everyone else gets ready to head back to Detaris and present what we've found to the elders there."

"Some of us will want to come with you, you know." Neritas grinned.

"And others will need to continue to guard the gate." Alitas stood. "The rest of us will guard you."

I blushed at this without being able to explain why. Thankfully this spurred everyone else to move on as well. Although I had expected some of them to disagree, none of them did. Instead, the dragons who wanted to come with me on my trip all came forward. It was easily over half of our group, and I almost laughed at how many were either protective of me or curious.

I'd expected Ben, Neritas, Flick, and Alitas. But my mother, Reijo, Jace, Tim, Harriet, Cios, Elias, Griffin, Merrik, Delphin, two other gate guards, and a city guard also wanted to join me.

"You are going to answer to Alitas or me for this mission," I said as soon as they'd all expressed their interest. "I appreciate that you all want to come with me, and you all have your own reasons, but I need to make sure we do this safely and we're going to be heading into an area that could still have a lot of shadow catchers in it and I don't know what was giving off this magical signature. There's a risk."

"Everything with you is a risk," Jace pointed out. "Let's just get it over and done with so I can stop being so curious about it and we can see if it helps us or not."

I almost laughed at her eagerness, but if I was being truthful, I was just as anxious. We hurried out to the boats, our drivers already resigned to having to come back for a second wave. As before, I knew it was more important for me to keep everyone safe, so I went in the first wave to shore, feeling for danger as we approached.

There was no sign of the shadow catchers, although I noticed two gate guards approaching as we approached the shore.

They went up to Alitas.

"Demons circled as you predicted through the night, almost as if they were patrolling. If they caught our scent or saw us, they pulled back a little until they felt bold enough to get close again," one of them reported.

I frowned, not liking what I was hearing. If they knew the demons had been on the prowl, why hadn't they told me? And most importantly, why couldn't I sense them now?

"Thank you. Keep an eye on them and what they do when we leave. Let me know if you think they're following us."

"Always." The gate guard hurried off before I could question him, but I took one thing from what I had heard already. I couldn't feel as far out as I wished when it came to the demons—this had confirmed it. If they had been circling me, they knew where I was.

While we waited for the rest of our group to come to shore as well, I sat down out of the way and closed my eyes. I focused, trying to reach out as far as I could, pushing myself and hoping it worked or was at least good practice. I didn't know if it would help much but I could only try.

No matter what I did, I couldn't feel any shadow catchers. I was soon interrupted by the others arriving, and it was time to get back on the road. Although I wasn't sure exactly where we were going, I felt confident being with Alitas and his team, and it was good to be doing something practical again.

Being stuck in the city had made me yearn for the ability to do something like this and feel as if my actions were making a difference. I liked *doing* rather than sitting around waiting.

Loading up into two cars and the van Cios liked to drive, we returned to the parking lot near the gate and unloaded again. Once more, I had everything important to me in the pack on my back, and I added extra snacks and water from the supplies in the vehicles, making sure no one else had to carry my load for me.

It was a heavy load, and it would have me aching again by the end of the day, but I couldn't leave any of it behind. It all mattered to me too much.

We trekked out of the parking lot, over the road, and found the exit to the overgrown path we'd found the day before. As we made our way down it, I tried to remember where we had joined it, but this was the part I was least sure of. It was hard for me to see that there had been a path here, let alone where to divert from it to find the underground tunnel.

After an hour, I wondered if we had gone too far. I

almost voiced my concerns, but Alitas never wavered, leading the way without stopping. Although it wasn't a harsh pace, the group began to tire, and no one spoke much as the hour wore on.

Thinking I needed to stop for one reason or another, I was about to call out to Alitas when he paused and looked off to one side of the path.

"There it is. We've come a little bit further along the path and it led around and into what must have once been a clearing."

"We could clear it out again," Delphin pointed out.

"Not yet," I replied. "Let's not make this any easier to be found until we have a better idea of what's here and if it's valuable. While random hikers probably won't find it, the same repellent atmosphere doesn't cover this side of the road."

This seemed to satisfy everyone, and we trooped across the long grasses and around the small trees toward the door to the underground tunnel system. When we reached it, I spotted the already trampled and squashed down area of the clearing around it and the way the roots had been moved to keep the trees alive but make the door easier to open, and was grateful for my decision. We'd already made it obvious enough that something was here.

I didn't want to tax my followers when we were in no danger, so we all rested for a few minutes. The whole way here I had tried to feel outward to the shadow catchers. I'd picked up on a few here and there, especially when we had parked, but I suspected I was having the same problem as always and my mental reach wasn't long enough. They could feel me, but I couldn't feel many of them.

A part of me wanted to give up entirely on this tracking business unless I could find a source of information on it or someone who might be able to teach it. But getting either form of help was likely impossible. There didn't appear to be any other red dragons anymore, and other than Anthony's journal and the book we'd found while looking for Reijo, there hadn't been anything that might explain what I could do or how to do it better.

This was something I needed to figure out for myself.

When we'd rested for about ten minutes, Alitas and Flick got up and approached the slab. Neritas followed, then several of the guards, until most of the men were standing there, working out the best way to get the slab of stone up and out of the position it was in so we could get underneath it again.

I was surprised that it was such a difficult task until I saw them attempt to get their hands underneath the edges and lift it.

"You need some leverage," Griffin suggested as he looked on. I suspected he feared being unable to contribute physically, and that his pride wouldn't let him get involved in the task.

I fought back a grin and looked around for something that might make a good long sturdy pole. Before I could go anywhere, Griffin presented the walking stick he had kept hold of since the previous morning. It was a good idea, and others grabbed theirs. Some of them had lost theirs along the way, like me, but several still had them.

With the strongest of the dragons using the sticks as levers and the rest of us helping wherever we could stand and get purchase, we lifted the slab again and managed to shift it to one side and prop it up, so the tunnel was open to the elements. It dislodged more dirt that cascaded into the room below, but Alitas was better prepared for it this time.

Two of the guards pulled buckets and spades from their packs and went inside first to clear the way a little and reveal the steps again.

I went with them, making myself glow before I reached out to the wall on the far side, where I could sense the magic. I noticed strange lines on the wall, so I connected to them with my mind. Almost immediately they started to glow like my sword and shield did. The light stretched down the tunnel we'd used, toward the tunnel that had collapsed inwards a little way down.

The lines from both these tunnels came onto the wall opposite the entrance and went around two sides and into the wall away from me, as if someone had bricked up a third passage in the same stone but not added the decoration.

"Well, if that's not some kind of obvious 'break through this and see what's on the other side,' I don't know what is," Jace noted when she joined me.

"Looks like we have some work to do." Ben rubbed his hands together as if he was excited at the challenge.

I was grateful that my friends were as enthusiastic as I was about opening this up and seeing what was on the other side. We all gathered around to see if we could work out how to get through.

"We almost need the shadow catchers' magic," Neritas suggested as he put his hands on it and tried to push it. It didn't budge.

He had a point. Something that could make it age and decay fast was going to be useful, and I was sure it would have worked if we had the time, but I wasn't luring a shadow catcher down here and throwing it at the wall enough times to get the job done. We would have to use more conventional means.

One of the dragons lifted his shovel and swung it by the spade end until the handle hit the wall. It left a dent but bent the handle as well. I covered my ears as the noise of the smack reverberated around the small room.

"Sorry." He looked a little sheepish.

"Not that way either." Putting my hands on my hips, I stared at the wall in our way and tried to think of a way I could wear it down. This was going to take a while.

CHAPTER TWENTY

After ten minutes of us scratching our heads and trying various things shy of smacking it again with something hard, I walked around the room to look for anything else unusual about it. I'd already played with the lighting a little and checked what magic I could feel.

Something was on the other side of this strange door, but getting through it was another matter. When I had thought of coming back here to see what we could find, I had expected to need to dig, and so Alitas had brought spades. We'd been so focused on getting out the previous afternoon that we hadn't taken in what material was in our way.

I could have kicked myself, knowing that the other dragons were waiting by the lake, expecting us to return soon. We'd already been gone a couple of hours, and the morning was dwindling away.

Although my look around the room was to appear as if I was doing something, I hoped it would give me an answer or solve my problem. When I had gone around the entire room and was right back at the door, though, my heart sank. I had nothing new.

"We might have to come back another time with more resources and a plan to get through." I realized it wasn't demeaning to admit that I didn't have all the answers and wouldn't always be perfect.

"I don't like not succeeding at things I try and do," Jace replied. "But you're calling the shots, Red. I won't deny that I'm also not loving standing here like an idiot. Before we go away and come stalking back with a whole bunch of shit to cut through rock, can you figure out what's on the other side anyhow?"

"You said that you could feel something magic," Alitas added when Jace moved to one side. "Can you tell what it is by connecting to it?"

My instinctive answer was no, but I stopped myself from uttering it and instead tilted my head to the side and thought about the query. Could I figure that out?

"Only one way to find out," I thought aloud and reached out to it with my mind. The feeling was faint, as if it was barely holding any charge. The briefest of sparks let me know something was there. A lesser dragon might have missed it entirely. I joined it, wondering what it could be.

Within seconds, it felt as if it was trying to pull energy out of me, almost painful in the way it latched onto the edge of my mind and hungrily pulled on my magic. Frowning, I tried to resist and managed to slow it down, but not stop the energy transfer altogether.

A moment later, I wobbled. My head was light as magic left me faster than I could recharge it. I didn't know what else to do but keep fighting it and reach out to my companions to take a little of their magic as well, assuming it would take a mix of colors.

I tried to think about this problem as if it was just another task I had to learn how to do. Slowly, I focused on squeezing off the supply and pulling myself back mentally from it.

This appeared to cause distress to everyone around me. I wasn't sure how they could notice what I was doing, but I knew I couldn't hurt them if this was dangerous.

I stopped drawing on the magic of everyone around me and relied on my own supply. Even that seemed to hurt, but I ignored it and let them all go. The second I properly disconnected from them, they all looked relieved. It made me feel a little better to have recognized their discomfort without anyone needing to point it out, and that I had stopped it already.

I still didn't have myself disconnected, and I didn't know what this discharge would do to me. As I stepped closer and tried again to hamper what it took out of me, it felt as if it had received too much. That was a feeling I wasn't used to, but as dizziness crept over me again, I was grateful it had slowed its demand.

Pretty sure that I was going to pass out before this thing filled up, I tried to fight it while also feeling for where the power might be going or what it might be doing. Slowly, I followed what appeared to be a ribbon of magic as it snaked out of whatever I was charging. I put a hand on the wall, dizzy but determined to carry on, and I felt it finally stop pulling magic from me.

Still somehow connected to it, but shaking and barely able to stand, I felt Neritas wrap an arm around my waist.

"I'm not sure you should try that again."

"It's done," I assured him as whatever I'd charged activated and pushed the energy out in a pulse that traveled closer to me. "Get back from the door."

The panicked warning in my voice had everyone moving back as I raised my shield and pulled on the magic in all of us to charge my shield and those of all the guards nearby.

There weren't many shields, and all of them together would prove inadequate to protect us if something exploded. All I could do was hope that wouldn't happen and that this was something else entirely. I had activated a magical item without knowing what it was or what it did.

Much to my delight and the amusement of most of the room, the stone covering the entrance swung open as if on well-greased hinges with no hint of a problem.

For a few seconds no one moved, and laughter filled the room.

"I guess that's what that item does when it's charged," I ventured once we were all calm. This almost set Jace off, but Neritas wasn't laughing, and neither was Alitas. I caught his gaze as I raised my eyebrow.

"It opened because a red dragon powered it from the outside, but just to be sure that whatever is in this room stays hidden from all but the most powerful red dragons, it latched onto you with magic and refused to let go of you until it had a significant amount of your magic," Alitas pointed out.

"And it was almost too much for you, Red," Neritas added.

"True, but it didn't finish me off, and we have it open

now. I'm just going to have to be a bit more careful in the future." I tried to smile as if I felt stronger than I did, but in truth they were both right and I had come close to having all the magic sucked out of me and more.

Foolish and a little too brave described me in that moment. Despite having suggested what had almost led to my ruin, Jace showed no guilt and was one of the first to look inside the room I'd opened up.

The walls were lit up in much the same way as the ones outside, the lines glowing and casting a faint glow over everything. It wasn't enough light to be thorough, however, just enough to show the edges of the room and the basics of what was inside.

Jace flicked her flashlight on and went to go in first but I put a hand out to stop her.

"If this room was as anti non-red dragon as it seemed, then it's probably a good idea I go first," I proposed as I took the first step.

Taking me by surprise, Jace stopped me, holding my arm gently before I could get too far ahead of her.

"I get the logic, but you're exhausted. You should draw a little magic from us and make sure you're strong again. That way if anything else in here wants to use you as a magic power supply, you'll have something to give it."

The suggestion had merit, but it was something I'd promised myself I would never do. To fill myself up at their expense felt wrong, but Jace appeared determined, her hand still on my arm.

Some of the other dragons who had heard her shuffled closer by way of consent to the idea. It wasn't easy, but I connected to them, making sure to exclude anyone who hadn't offered directly, and drew on their energy just enough to feel as if I was strong again.

Although I wasn't topped up all the way, I hadn't been when I had been tested by whatever had opened the door either. It was a strange feeling to take so much from all of them, but I had nine willing dragons and didn't fill all the way up.

When I was done, I gave my attention back to the room ahead and took a few more steps inside. I didn't feel anything else out of the ordinary, but I did make the room brighter by lighting up the lines more and finding some wooden pillars that I could also get to glow.

As the room came into view, I took in what was there. It appeared to be an armory. Along several of the walls were rows of shields, spears, and swords, and all of them were similar to the ones Alitas and I bore. They were identical to the one Neritas carried. In the middle of the room was a bench of other items that I didn't entirely recognize, with a single exception.

My mother noticed them at the same time I did and exclaimed as she went to the healing devices that sat on one section of the table. I grinned and took one, and handed her another for backup.

"Everyone, time to kit up." I finally felt as if this diversion of mine had been entirely worth it.

I didn't need to tell any of them twice. Griffin even chose a shield and a shorter spear that would suit him as a walking stick as well. He slid the shield onto his arm, his eyes glinting in the light reflecting off it, and he tested the spear exactly like a walking stick as he moved around the room and came back my way.

When he reached me and stopped, I put my hands out and touched both objects, feeding some energy into them and charging them so they could be used in battle against demons.

"There, now you'll be a force in battle."

"That's something I've not been in a very long time." His voice cut out a little as if the admission had made him emotional.

With his chosen items charged up, the others came to me as well. Jace grinned ear-to-ear as I put magic in the sword she'd chosen, chainmail and the buckler she'd opted to pair it with.

Before long, my mother stood beside me helping to power everything up. We didn't fill it all entirely, as neither of us wanted to be completely drained of magic when we still had a lot of the day left to power through. It still seemed like the right thing to do to equip everyone in this way, and by the time we were done and heading back out of the armory the atmosphere had shifted entirely.

If I had felt as if I was forming an army before, I really felt it now. Alitas and some of the others picked up some spare items and more healing devices for other members of the gate guards and my honor guards, including Kryos.

I made sure to get one of each item on the bench before me, grabbing little brooches, rings, amulets, and all sorts of other things. I had no idea what most of them did, but we could discover that later when I had more time to focus on them one by one. My pack was considerably heavier than when we'd arrived.

"You should close the door on all of this again if you can," Alitas suggested.

The charge from the door opening had gone somewhere, but I didn't know where, and with all the powered-up items near me it was almost impossible to work out what was what.

"Can you get everyone to go outside so I can feel for it without so much magical interference?" I asked Alitas before I closed my eyes to focus.

In the background I heard him encouraging everyone to do as I asked, and the area slowly cleared. Some only hung back and gave me space, and I felt the magic signature of the items they carried still in the room with me.

Amused and comforted by how persistent some of them were at keeping me safe, I relaxed a little. I was wary that this next task would be as difficult as opening the door had been, but I had hopes that it wouldn't. Locking something was almost always easier than unlocking it.

With my mind, I searched for something to connect to that wasn't an item in the room itself. I couldn't detect anything with charge in there, but I kept feeling farther outward and searching around in what I thought was a spiral from the original point that had opened the door.

The seconds ticked by as the pressure mounted and still nothing jumped out at me.

"Try the door itself," Neritas said a minute or so in.

His voice was gentle, but it still made me jump and lose my focus a moment. There was wisdom in his words, however. If the charge had traveled to the door, perhaps the door itself held the answer to me shutting it again.

I felt around inside for something magical to connect to, finally finding a connection near one wall in what might have been the hinges. As soon as I connected to it, it sent a wave of energy toward me and almost drowned me in raw power. Staggering back, I almost fell over.

Neritas caught me as I opened my eyes in time to see the door swing shut. No sooner had it done so than the faint magical beacon inside the room came back. This time I knew better than to connect with it, and I withdrew my mind.

Still feeling a little overwhelmed by the magic the door had flung back at me when it sealed shut, I reached out to everyone and all the items I could feel again and pumped it toward everything and everyone until I had shared the love a little.

It was a heady feeling of a different type, to be able to give it back to all of them and not feel tired afterward, as if the magic had grown while it had been stored in the door and now the weapons and us were supercharged.

Either way, this trip had been worth every single minute, and I was going back to the group with proof that I had made the right decision and that I was a red dragon who could get stuff done.

CHAPTER TWENTY-ONE

By the time we met back up with the other dragons in our party, they were waiting on the shore of the lake. The yacht was in the distance looking tempting in the early afternoon sun.

Although everyone else was eager to get going again, I forced them to halt while those of us who had been out all morning had some lunch, and we shared around the kit we'd brought for the others.

Not all of the dragons were thrilled at what we'd brought back. The other city guards didn't take anything and almost seemed suspicious of it. I chalked it up to not having Capricia there to tell them something was okay for them to have or do.

Though we'd brought back as much as we could, everything was soon claimed except the items that had unknown uses in my bag, stashed away from prying eyes. Until I knew what they did and how easy they were to operate, I wasn't letting anyone near them.

As soon as we'd finished eating, everyone was eager to

get going again, especially Griffin and the gate guards. They were right to be anxious. We had gathered lots of evidence, as well as some equipment and knowledge, and now it was time to return all that to Detaris and figure out what to do next.

I hoped the elders in the city would appreciate the danger now, after everything I had done to prove it while trying to protect everyone. Griffin had been convinced that something needed to be done and that I was already on the right path, and hopefully that would mean something to the rest of the elders.

Of course, just because they might agree with us, it didn't mean the population of the city would be as charitable. They had attacked me even after the elders had accepted that I was going to take the throne.

While we were packing up the cars, it became clear that I had more people with me than the day I'd left, so we packed the van full and redistributed the luggage a little. I'd expected some of them to want to drive off to other places, but they all wanted to come with me, even Elias and Sarai.

A part of me questioned the logic of showing up at the dragon city with a bunch of dragons who were considered terrorists, but when I stood to one side of the path and considered them as people, I knew they were goodhearted, and allies I had come to respect.

I stood for a few minutes, feeling outward and getting the sense that the demons were out there waiting for something. Ben studied me for a few seconds.

"You're worried. And I don't like it when you're worried." He leaned in closer to me so I could talk without being overheard.

I told him some of the fears that were weighing down my mind and adding butterflies to my stomach. How we had a lot of dragons teamed with us who weren't understood very well.

"There's a chance that it will make our role harder to play, but it may also make people realize how serious all this is if there are leaders from different groups all rallying to you. They make convincing allies for anyone who knows their history."

"Or off-putting."

"Only time will tell, but there is little point worrying about it. We can't change it now and we can only go forward. Any single dragon who realizes that what we are trying to do is worth fighting for could make a difference right now. It's more power the next time we make a journey to the gate and it's a sign that you're getting through to some people even if you're not getting through to everyone."

Ben had a point, but I still felt anxious as we got into the cars and drove away from the area and the shadow catchers that appeared to be watching and waiting. I wished I understood their strategy.

I was in the front car once again, but this one was driven by Alitas, and Griffin no longer rode beside the captain of the city guard, but the captain of my honor guard instead. It felt strange and somehow right all at the same time. In a lot of ways, it was an upgrade. But it made me wonder how the city dragons would perceive it.

As we got closer and closer to the city, my unease and anxiety about the reactions of the antagonistic dragons such as Brenta and Capricia, and memories of the many times I had been attacked there grew. It made my stomach knot and my body feel on edge. It was silly, and I wanted to tell myself off for my lack of maturity. After all the times I had fought the shadow catchers and been hounded by them, I would have expected to be anxious and feel fear when leaving the city, not when going to it.

But something about the demons was predictable and easy to overcome. I'd defeated them many times and had good allies whom I could rely on. By contrast, the city residents were unpredictable and cruel. They also had a lot more power over my future that I couldn't combat. When someone decided they didn't like you, there wasn't much you could do about it.

I couldn't convince my body it was okay when it didn't think it was. I was stuck feeling as if I was heading into a place that was detrimental to my health. It already had been—I still hurt from the last attack there.

Trying to think of anything but the city, I reached out with my mind for anything around me. It wasn't something I normally did while driving, because shadow catchers couldn't keep up with a car and it wasn't as if they could drive. The practice would do me good, though, and who knew, maybe I'd pick up on a stray here and there and confirm that they were simply everywhere and not following and hounding me specifically.

Now and then I thought I felt something behind us, but it wasn't the same feeling as a shadow catcher and soon went away again. Briefly, I wondered if it was us passing places the demons had influence over or where they'd set up camp, especially when now and then I also felt shadow catchers that were stationary somewhere near the road we were on.

The feelings grew more frequent as we traveled, making it clear that there were plenty of shadow catchers in the wild, but they concentrated near places dragons lived. It made sense, and I could have kicked myself for not thinking of trying it sooner.

As we reached the cliffside road and were close to the turning into the city and the section where we were would appear to drive off a cliff, I expected Alitas to need someone else to lead the way, but he drove it as confidently as Ben had, taking the turn and not flinching when it looked like we were driving off the edge.

I knew I'd never get used to it, but I appreciated the view as the city appeared, all tall towers and glistening rock. For a moment I marveled at it, grateful for its existence, but then I realized it was crunch time. The last time I had returned here, Neritas had declared me queen and I had been forced to deal with the consequences. Though I had been intending to do something similar, I hadn't been sure, and it still weighed on my mind that he had taken the decision away from me.

Of course, he had apologized, quick to see that it might not have been the wisest action or manner to do it, and I had forgiven him. Despite that, I still had to deal with the consequences of those actions.

No differently than every arrival of mine, dragons flew in to greet us or show curiosity as we all pulled up and parked. I was coming back with far more dragons than I'd left with, something that also seemed to be a habit.

Unlike previous occasions, when we got out of the car

there wasn't a group to welcome us back or guards who came to greet us. Instead, Capricia landed, transformed, and started a line of city guards that spread out across the path to the rest of the city. She held her shield and stood in the middle, blocking the way.

"I'm glad you're safe," I said as soon as I got out, trying to ignore how hostile her reaction felt. I was sure that Griffin would be able to sort it out.

As if to make a point that I was back from a task an elder had asked me to achieve, I opened his car door and offered him my arm to help him out of the car. He took it, a frown flitting across his face as he took in the situation.

Capricia didn't reply to either of us, but she glared at me as my group formed up. More dragons landed, and I heard gasps and murmurs as they realized who some of the dragons in my entourage were, especially when Alitas, Elias, and Sarai got out of the cars.

"I'd like to head to the chamber right away," Griffin requested as he approached Capricia and the line of guards. None of them moved, and Capricia simply studied him.

Capricia looked at the city guards with us and ignored Griffin. "Guards, get back to your posts."

"What's going on?" I asked, not surprised when they all obeyed her and were the only ones allowed through the line and away from us.

"I'm doing my job," she replied. It was cryptic enough that I felt tension rising as I grew angrier. I didn't like this one bit, and it was clear that we weren't meant to.

"Your job is to protect the dragons of this world, and we have information that's needed for that purpose." I stepped closer and kept my voice low so the whole city wouldn't hear our exchange.

"No. My job is to protect this city and carry out the wishes of the elders within it."

I raised an eyebrow and stepped back as Griffin came forward as well. This wasn't the greeting we'd expected, and the knot in my stomach tightened.

"And I am an elder in this city. Stand down, Capricia, and let me and these people past." Griffin puffed out his chest a little and raised his chin as if this would give him the authority he needed. "We need to talk to the other elders about everything we've seen. You left before we saw the most important aspects."

Capricia studied the shorter elder as if she was considering what he was asking of her. A moment later, Brenta walked out of the crowd. Capricia moved to the side to let Brenta join the line, although the elder stayed behind the large line of shields they wielded.

"A vote was held yesterday afternoon on Capricia's return. You're no longer an elder of this city."

"You took a hearing on my status without me? That goes against the normal order of things. I should be allowed to defend myself and hear the reasons if nothing else."

"None of us have anything against telling you the reasons."

The panic and unease grew inside me.

When I looked around the group and saw the look on my mother's face, I realized some of what I felt wasn't just the situation unfolding in front of us. There were shadow catchers coming. Lots of them. And I felt a handler or two among them.

"We have a firsthand witness who has informed us that you have been compromised mentally by the enemy and your judgment can no longer be trusted."

"That's a load of—"

"I hate to interrupt this," I stepped forward as the feeling of unease grew. "But we have a bigger problem. There are demons on the way. Lots of them."

Capricia laughed at this, and no one else seemed to react as Brenta looked at her and back to us.

"We thought you would try something like this. Being the hero, or even setting them on us if we didn't agree with you. Tell me, when did you sell your soul to the demon?" Brenta looked right at me as she asked the question.

I didn't respond, so shocked to be asked that I couldn't process it. How could anyone think I was in league with the demons? I kept risking my life fighting them.

"Leave now and you can leave peacefully," Capricia added, and I watched the entire line of guards stiffen as if they were prepared to attack or defend the line.

"You don't understand. There's a small army of shadow catchers coming. And even if we flew up and over them, they would still come and attack all of you."

"And if you continue to threaten us, we will attack you."

"It's not a threat. I don't control them, nor am I in league with them."

"So you say, but it's clear that you are and have been from the beginning. You've been undermining us from the inside out." Capricia set her jaw as she glared at me.

I looked back at the dragons near me. They were all

concerned and looking to me for orders. Each one of them was here because of me in one way or another.

I had no idea what to do. We could leave, all of us fly away and go somewhere safer, but it would leave the city with no one to defend it. I didn't doubt that with no red dragons, the city would take a beating. Even if they pulled up everything and hid in their towers, it wasn't a foolproof defense plan. There were bridges, and with handlers, someone could get inventive and get the shadow catchers to the towers.

With the small army of demons coming, dragons would die if we left.

But the longer I stood in front of the city, the more angry and aggressive the dragons in Detaris became. We couldn't stay where we were either, or they would attack.

Somehow I had to figure out what to do with no good option.

Somehow I needed to find the right moral answer. The answer my conscience could live with no matter what the outcome of my choice.

CHAPTER TWENTY-TWO

I stepped back toward the group I'd arrived with, and Griffin reluctantly came back away from the line with me. I needed to buy some time and I needed to make sure the people near me were safe.

"Griffin, Elias, and Sarai, you should take a couple of guards and fly out of here. Get somewhere safe." I looked at the weaker elders and knew that no matter what followed, they needed to be safe.

"If you think you're going to stand here and fight a battle on both sides and send us away to watch or only hear about it afterward, you're very much mistaken." Elias lifted the shield he'd taken from the group spoils earlier, and Sarai pulled out a set of daggers she'd hidden about her body.

"We've been fighting these demons longer than you've been alive," Sarai added.

"And if these two are staying and fighting, I'm certainly not running away." Griffin's eyes shone with a determined light. "I might not have fought anything before, but I can hold a shield and I can aid those who know better where to stab. And no matter what, this city is a place I've protected my whole life. They don't understand what's coming, do they?"

"No, I don't think they do." I wasn't sure I did either.

It was hard to know anything right now, but I looked around at the group I'd arrived with and knew they were with me, every single one of them. And we wanted to defend Detaris if we could.

I turned and faced Capricia again. "We're not going anywhere. We won't come any closer, but you're in danger and whether you believe us or not, we're here to defend this city."

"And we don't want your defense. We don't want any of you here at all. Many of you are already banished, and from this moment on, the rest of you are as well," Brenta declared.

I frowned but didn't respond. It wasn't anything new. Given how they were reacting to us already, I thought it was a given. Was this them blustering because they didn't know what else to do?

"Leave, before we make you." Capricia almost growled the last word, and her line moved forward with her.

"We'll leave once these demons are dealt with and you're safe. Don't be stupid, Capricia. You know what these creatures can do. You've seen them in battle and know what they'll do to the city in the numbers that are coming."

"We only have your word for the latter, and even if I believed that so many were coming, they always follow you. It's you controlling them. You're the handler."

I shook my head but didn't bother to speak again. It was futile.

Before I could figure out how to defuse the situation so that we could stay and fight, Ben, Neritas, Flick, Griffin, and everyone else who had been a citizen of the city until a few minutes ago stepped up beside me.

"Brenta, think about this," Ben said. "You've led this city as an elder for a long time. Has there ever been a red dragon handler before? Have so many ever been suckered in by one? Look at the dragons before you. You may not agree with all of them, but many of us have lived alongside you for a long time. We're telling you that Scarlet is speaking the truth. We've seen evidence and we have proof. Let us show you."

Despite Ben's reasonable response, Brenta shook her head and Capricia lifted her sword.

"This is your last warning." The city guard captain took another small step. "Leave now, or we will use force."

"Then you'll have to use force." The rest of my group backed up, but I stayed there, alone. "You'll have to be the first to strike a fellow dragon who is standing here offering you nothing but protection and aid. Go on, show everyone which one of us is willing to do anything to get what they want."

I met Capricia's gaze, and no one dared move or speak. I knew they were all waiting for either her or I to make the first move, but I'd called her bluff. If she truly believed I was a serious threat to the city, she would attack now. Otherwise it would be obvious they were trying to control the city for other reasons.

I had no idea what they might be trying to achieve, but I knew I wasn't lying.

"You really don't get it, do you? We can't trust a word you say." Capricia raised her sword and before I could move, she and all the guards rushed to attack.

With no other option, I fell back to the group. We held the line, bringing up charged shields and keeping our weapons down.

"Defend but try not to hurt them," I yelled. "At least until the demons get here."

It was a tall order when so many city guards were attacking, but I kept out a little ahead of my friends and charged a line across the ground. Although it seemed underhanded of me, I drew on the magic of the city guards to do it.

While I didn't want them to get hurt, I wasn't going to make it easy for them to hurt me, and if that meant I used their own magic against them, so be it. It would save the magic of my own dragons for fighting the shadow catchers when they showed up.

As Capricia reached me, she tried to stab past my shield, but I pushed her attack aside with my shield. Energy transferred from it, up her sword and into her arm, seeming to zap her.

She cried out and dropped the weapon. I felt bad, but she recovered as the guard next to her tried to swing a mace at my head. I ducked, and Neritas caught the swing with his shield instead. It made him step to one side slightly, sending him off balance for a moment.

I reached for him as I stood again, and Capricia used the opportunity to try to smack me back down. Her shield came at me with her whole body behind it. I barely had time to react, but Ben stepped in from my other side and caught the edge of her shield, turning it away with a loud bang.

Wincing, because it sounded like it hurt both of them, I reached to control her shield with my mind, also feeling her pumping her magic into the crowd around her. I used her magic and that of the black dragons to counteract it, drawing more from them and adding a little of my own to see if I could fight them in their own arena.

Although I wasn't successful at trying to calm them instead of inciting them to anger, I was pretty sure I was weakening the shield Capricia carried.

She roared at me in anger and charged again, and I decided to test my theory. As she put her weight behind the shield again, I turned my hardened magical shield edge-on against it and held firm.

With a louder bang, her shield split in two. My shield went through and cut into her arm underneath. She screamed in pain as I tried to pull back and away from her. I hadn't intended to hurt her, but it looked as if this fight wasn't going to end any other way.

Hers was the first injury on either side, and this stirred the pot and instigated the wrath of the city in a way it hadn't yet been. Several dragons launched themselves off the nearby towers as Capricia was pulled back by others to get her medical aid.

I felt guilty, but only so much. She was using her magic to make the city angry at us, and now I was dealing with the guards who were acting out of that emotion. In a lot of ways, she was to blame for this fight.

A dragon swooped overhead, claws outstretched as they tried to attack us from the air. Everyone was forced to duck, and the guards then took the opportunity to push us all back a little.

I growled, using my shield to defend Neritas from another attack he didn't see coming. Although the city guards had the numbers, and other citizens were stepping in to aid them, my group was mostly seasoned fighters, all of them having fought shadow catchers in some capacity, and we were used to working together.

Despite that advantage, it was still a hard fight, and I grew more and more concerned that this wasn't going to end until a lot of dragons were hurt. Every minute we spent fighting here, we weren't preparing for the wave of demons coming in, and my group would be caught between the two. Would the city stop fighting us when a bigger threat arrived?

As another dragon swooped down toward us, I moved close to Neritas, and Flick came closer as well.

"Cover us," I instructed Flick as I grabbed Neritas.

"Lift me as that dragon flies by," I called over the sounds of fighting.

I wasn't sure he'd heard me as he blocked another attack and Flick moved into my space in the line against the city, but he turned to me, grabbed me around the waist, and with more strength than I'd have thought possible, he threw me up into the air right as the dragon flew over.

Not only did I hit it with my shield, but I stabbed at the nearest claw with my sword as well. It was time to send a clear message: I would defend the dragons with me.

Both strikes did damage, and the dragon screeched,

veered away, and clipped its right wing on a tower before it was forced to land on a bridge and morph back into human form.

The hit knocked me back and I turned as gravity caught up with me. Somehow Neritas caught me again, moving to the side and getting his arms underneath my back before I hit the ground. With a quick flick of one arm and a lowering of the other, he got me upright again and I steadied myself on my feet.

"Thanks," I said.

I had no opportunity to do or say more as the fighting from so many sources and the persistence of the city guards started to break through our line and push us into pockets. I fought to push back the few guards nearest us, using my shield as a battering ram and breaking a couple more of their shields entirely.

At the same time, I felt the shadow catchers approaching the top of the ridge behind us. Shrieks from above and calls of many voices confirmed that city dwellers were finally seeing the demons and how many of them there were. I tried not to worry about it and focus on the dragons in front of me as Capricia rejoined the fight with her arm bandaged and a new shield in her hand.

"Stop this now," I yelled at her, but I wasn't sure she heard me as the dragons closest to me ignored my call as well.

Once again, a dragon descended. It took me by surprise, and Neritas wasn't close enough to throw me up to it. Someone else anticipated it, however— Cios copied what Neritas had done, and Jace was in the air.

Although she had an armory shield and sword, she did

a similar amount of damage as I had done, catching the dragon on the chest with the shield and raking her sword down a leg as it flew by.

It forced the other dragons to reconsider attacking us from the air, a reprieve we desperately needed. This was chaos, and I still hoped it could be stopped before it went much further. I looked for Capricia and reached for a magical connection, and felt her fueling the rage around me.

I did everything I could to combat it, despite not being as skilled at emotional manipulation as she was, and continued to push back at any guards who came close.

My group focused on disarming and breaking shields before letting the scared dragons retreat. It wasn't a great strategy, because many of them came back with fresh supplies, but this couldn't go on forever. In a minute or two we were going to have to fight on two fronts.

The demons had arrived.

CHAPTER TWENTY-THREE

With my mind almost collapsing under the horrible feeling of so many shadow catchers and handlers this close, I had to pull back my reach a little and focus on the magic and connection I felt.

At the same time, my group tried to fall back a little. It gave us the advantage of being spread out across a narrower section of land, making it easier for us to defend against our attackers in both directions, but it also put us in a slight dip and made the fight harder on us from both sides.

The city dragons weren't letting up, even when they noticed what was coming.

"Capricia," I called, trying to get her attention, still hoping to resolve this with words. She didn't respond, if she'd even heard me over the din.

Out of time to stop one fight over the other, I turned and helped form a line with Elias, Sarai, and most of Jace's folks fighting the shadow catchers as they did their best. I charged the ground in several places, finally pulling on some of the magic from my own group although I still pulled what I could from the city dragons who were close enough.

If we were going to defend their city, they were at least going to help us. I lashed out at the first shadow catcher that got past all the charged lines, catching its beak with my shield and slashing underneath as I pushed it up and away.

The attack finished it off and allowed me to turn and hit another. Smoke rose from its wound. With a strong start and adrenaline already coursing through us, we dealt with most of the first wave in seconds, and vapor formed in a thick cloud above us all.

I pulled back as I heard a guard yelp. Turning, I saw Reijo stabbing one in the shoulder as it tried to knock my mother over.

Roaring in anger at seeing my only living relative being attacked so relentlessly, I charged back toward the guard and hit him in the side with my shield. Instant remorse hit me when I heard his bones crunch as he went flying. He was on the ground, struggling to breathe. I'd crushed his ribs on one side, but as long as he survived I knew the guilt would quickly fade. If he lived, he would heal. My mother was hurt too, and Reijo helped her off the ground as I heard another angry yell.

Capricia had seen what I'd done and was storming toward me.

"This needs to stop," I shouted. I turned and raised my shield to stand my ground against her. "We should be fighting the demons, not each other."

"You are the demon," she screamed as she ran at me.

I blocked her attack, and our shields clashed again, but she'd gathered so much speed as she came down the hill toward me that the force knocked me back a step anyway. Trying to recover, I stabbed forward. She easily dodged and thrust back.

I moved the shield in the way in time to avoid being skewered. She growled as the charge ran up her weapon and shocked her again, but she didn't drop it this time or do anything but grit her teeth against the pain.

We dueled for another minute or two, both of us looking for openings but neither of us finding them. The whole time I pulled magic from Capricia, trying to fight her ability. I didn't doubt that she was fueling this fight. She'd made the citizens and the guard angrier than I had ever seen them. And given they had already attacked me and beaten me to a pulp, that was saying something.

With the fighting raging on around us, the lines fell apart, and shadow catchers got through our line of defense to attack anyone else within reach. City guards were forced to defend the city and fight beside us, but the chaos led to dragons getting hurt. I needed to wake Capricia up, somehow.

I had to disarm her again and force her to talk, calmly, and open her eyes to what was going on around us. I pulled on all the magic I needed, taking it from anyone not currently on my side of the fight or fighting a shadow catcher and using it to make her sword and shield brittle. I shocked her a few times as I hit her again.

She fought through it longer than I expected before her sword shattered. Slivers of the metal went flying, and one of them buried itself in my shield and another in my arm, making me yelp as well.

When she realized it could do no more, Capricia threw the hilt at me. It bounced off my shield, and we ran at each other. It was time to end this.

As she attacked again, I made her shield as brittle as possible. It also broke apart, and she threw the part left in her hands at me. This time it caught me in the face and stunned me for half a second.

I shrugged it off but not before she grabbed a rock and threw it at me. Blocking that with the shield as well, I noticed the bandage on her arm was showing blood and she was slowing, panting, her eyes wide.

I drew more magic from her, and I knew she wouldn't be able to hold up much longer.

The fighting spirit in her didn't let her give up when it looked like she was going to be defeated. She threw herself toward me again. I turned to one side as I sheathed my sword and let her fly past. Instead of taking note of the position of the shadow catcher near us, she whirled and came at me again.

This time I had a free hand, and I grabbed her good arm, spun her, stuck out my foot and tripped her over onto her back. As she hit the ground so hard it winded her, I held my shield so it was over her neck and would cut off her head if she so much as moved.

"I am not your enemy." I let all the anger and frustration I felt pour into my words as I held her in place. "Look around you."

Shifting just enough so that she could turn her head, I let her do just that and thankfully she listened. I felt her let go of the magic and stop pouring anger into the dragons around her.

Following her gaze, I saw her take in all the shadow catchers as they attacked her dragons and mine alike, but mostly I let her see the two handlers standing on the ridge, controlling the destruction.

"If we don't direct our forces, those two are going to see this city destroyed and there won't be anything left for you to defend. Whatever you think of me, I would rather be fighting them than you. Got it?"

Capricia didn't reply, but I saw the concern in her eyes as a city guard squealed, hit in the side by a shadow catcher.

"Help me," I pleaded again as I pulled my shield away and ran at the shadow catcher. I barreled into it, knocking it back and saving the city guard's life.

He drew his sword as I drew mine, but Capricia ran up as well. "Fight them, not her, or Detaris will fall."

His eyes went wide, but none of us had time to do anything else as the creature attacked and another joined it. Capricia had nothing left to defend or fight with, but Sarai was nearby and flicked one of her daggers around to hold out the hilt.

"You're giving that back when this is all done, or I swear I'll tear this entire city down to get it back." Sarai pointed at me. "Her grandfather gave me this pair and charged them so well they've been killing these demons my whole life.

"I'll charge them back up when this is over if you kill a bunch more today." I grinned as I stabbed at another demon.

"Deal, but I'd have sent these monsters back to hell either way."

This made all three of us chuckle and then Capricia was helping me again, hitting the shadow catcher as I herded it away from the still-vulnerable guard.

"Help fight the demons," Capricia yelled the second it was dead and she had a breather to think again. "Stop fighting other dragons. Now isn't the time."

I gave a similar command to my own team and the impact was almost immediate, as everyone who wasn't already fighting a shadow catcher started working with the dragons around them to do so. For a moment I stood back, letting Sarai and Jace issue battle commands while I reached for the magic of all the dragons left with any to give and charged weapons and shields across the entire battlefield.

Feeling my mother do the same, I watched her fall back behind Reijo, Cios, and Tim, who had been fighting beside her the last little while. Knowing they were a solid unit, I felt relief when Sarai and Jace got the remaining shadow catchers close to the city dealt with and a line formed for everyone to fall into.

Capricia took the shield from the injured city guard and sent him back to get first aid. I threw my healing device toward him, charging it partially as it went.

"Get someone to use that on you," I instructed, knowing I probably wouldn't see it again but hoping the goodwill gesture would be remembered by the dragons. There were more where it had come from, but only so many.

With that done and Neritas, Flick, Jace, Ben, and Capricia coming closer, I realized I had fully formed my usual fighting team and we could power through pretty much anything. My only concern was that I had already almost fully drained Capricia in my attempt to stop her, not that she had been idle with her magic.

Now that she wasn't trying to make everyone around her as angry at me as she was, the atmosphere was far calmer and one of determined resistance against a common enemy.

"Want to go take out another handler?" Capricia asked as our group helped the line solidify with more dragons getting into place.

Momentarily distracted by another couple of dragons running up with older equipment, which I charged and hoped would hold up, I took a moment to consider her proposal.

"They're going to hide behind their shadow catchers and pull back if we get close," I guessed.

"We could get a dragon to fly us in closer and drop right on their heads," Neritas suggested. "If I can throw you at a dragon to fight, a dragon can drop us on one of them."

He had a point, but it would mean a dragon flying out of the city, away from its protection, and also possible exposure to the human world. No one in the city was going to like the idea. The elders were already angry enough that I kept bringing attention to the magical realm in one way or another.

"We'd need someone who can really fly," Ben said. "And not one of you three."

I grinned as he pointed at Neritas, Flick, and me. We were great at flying, but we all needed to be in human form for this to work. Our entire unit did. It was going to be dangerous, and we ran the risk of being overwhelmed if we weren't careful once we took on the handlers.

"We need a brave dragon to fly," I called, not sure how many would respond when the city had been almost entirely against me only minutes earlier, but Jared flew down and landed in human form a second later.

"What do you need me to do?" He had not an ounce of hesitation on his face.

Capricia quickly explained while I worked with the rest of the group to skewer another shadow catcher and send it into a puff of smoke. It was quickly dealt with when all of us could work together. We retreated, getting the other dragons to hold the line again.

The handlers were bringing more shadow catchers toward wherever they thought the line was weakest, but I met the gaze of one of them for a moment. I stared the creature down. It was hard to tell if it was someone who had once been human, as the shape was only vaguely humanoid.

I had no idea if they knew what was about to happen, but they were confident, and if nothing else that made me want to take the fight to them. It was time I took control of this fight rather than reacting to what was happening.

With an entire city of dragons, we should be able to defeat this many shadow catchers, but I felt more turning up all the time. This attack had been planned. If nothing else, it also explained all the monsters I had sensed and how many more of them there had been the closer I had gotten to the city.

I'd assumed this was normal instead of wondering if it had been a warning sign. The troops had been heading in for a fight and I'd completely missed it. Had I known then what I did now, I'd have acted differently.

There was no point dwelling on what could have been when I was in the middle of a fight for the here and now. Once everyone was safe and this battle dealt with, I could figure out what to learn from it and beat myself up mentally over things I couldn't have changed anyway.

Capricia continued talking to Jared as we fought, his part in the plan more complicated. I slowly fed her a little magic from other sources, drawing it from the dragons around us who seemed to have plenty.

"You're all crazy and brave in a way that most aren't, but it seems those two often go hand in hand," Jared remarked once he had heard what we wanted to do. "But I'll do it. And I'll join you on the other end if someone will get me one of those fancy swords and shields."

"You don't have to join us," I replied, mostly because I had no idea where I could get another sword and shield, but then Merrik threw his over.

"I can fight as easily with a spear and a plank of wood. I've done it many a time." Merrik grinned and flicked me a wink. I didn't approve, but another city guard ran up with a spare set of city gear and Merrik took that instead while I charged it up as best I could.

The city weaponry didn't hold magic in the same way, so I had to keep charging it all. I wouldn't be able to do that as easily once we went through with our plan, but with any luck I'd swing this battle and the shadow catchers would stop for at least a moment when their handlers died.

Of course, this could go horribly wrong and the city and all of us could be overwhelmed. We were dividing ourselves as much as trying to divide them. But our group hadn't failed yet, and that gave me hope.

"Okay, everyone ready?" We all came together and Jared transformed back into a dragon, filling up the space beside us.

"Ready as we'll ever be. Lead us into battle, Red." Neritas grinned as if this was the best adventure yet.

CHAPTER TWENTY-FOUR

It worried me that Jared might be feeling weighed down as the group of us climbed onto his back as swiftly as we could. We all sat sideways with our backs to someone else's and our arms linked so no one would fall off the side, but in a way that we could all drop off as soon as I gave the signal. In our spare hands we all held our shields.

I was near the front to try to gauge the best moment to drop and also hoping that Jared could make this as easy as possible by getting low. He couldn't get too low, however, or they would be able to hurt him.

Although he'd spoken of joining us, I wasn't sure if he'd fly off and then come back to land with us or if he planned to transform, but either way, we had to be ready.

The shadow catchers and their handlers noticed that we were up to something, and we had to go. Jared leaped into the air, and the first powerful downbeat of his wings almost knocked us all off.

"Steady, everyone. This won't work if we lose anyone."

"Don't worry, Red. We're going to stick to you like

glue," Flick assured me. "We're not letting you get the credit for being a crazy-ass red dragon without being able to point out there was a dragon of every color doing this with you."

"I'm not sure that says what you think it does about your intellect." I grinned as Jared quickly took us across the land, heading straight for the enemy.

We didn't get much longer to think about it, as we flew so fast that we were almost overhead within seconds. I was about to jump off and call for the others to do the same when Jared transformed in midair and we all dropped right in front of the handlers with Jared in the center of the group.

I pulled my sword as shadow catchers came rushing at us and the handlers tried to fall back.

"Guard my red ass." I rushed toward the nearest handler and slashed at the air in front of him. I charged the ground behind him and around him, forming a semicircle of danger to keep him from running away.

Facing me with wide eyes and letting out a hissing noise akin to an angry cat's, he stepped back, right onto a patch I'd powered up. His foot smoked as he yowled and came forward again.

"You're not going anywhere." I struck at him again.

He dodged once more, and a shadow catcher came darting in from my side. Neritas and Flick got there before anyone else could, and I continued to focus on the demon in front of me.

Realizing he had no choice but to fight for his life, the handler produced a blade, seeming to draw the weapon from an invisible sheath. I blocked and heard a strange noise as it hit my shield. The metal heated against my skin, almost to the point of pain before a thrust from me forced him back.

I made a mental note to dodge more than block and charged more of the land around us, hemming him into a smaller and smaller area as we fought on. Unlike Fintar, who had been part human, this handler appeared to be something else entirely and fought in a different way. He wasn't fully corporeal, and when I did hit him with my blade, it didn't do as much damage as it could do to a shadow catcher.

Still, I carried on fighting, reminding myself that I had to win this. The city depended on me making this battle far easier.

Twice more I was almost hit. The demon was so fast that it took everything I'd learned to anticipate his moves.

"You might want to hurry this up, Red," I heard Jace call from behind me somewhere. "More and more of these demons are trying to get to you."

I gritted my teeth, noticing that the handler had backed off as much as he could, trying to buy time until he could overwhelm me with his minions. If I didn't change things up, my friends were going to be overrun.

Wanting to wipe what looked like a smug grin on my enemy's face, I charged, using the shield as a weapon once more and bashing and attacking with both items, stepping forward and getting within my enemy's reach and swing.

He was unable to recover from each blow before I landed the next. Pushing him back onto charged land, I kept going, yelling my rage, fear, and frustrations against these creatures with every hit. It was passionate and relied on my muscles remembering what to do in a way that I normally didn't.

Most of the blows landed, and the creature recoiled until it was finally on its last legs. I felt its control on the shadow catchers waver before it collapsed, and I ran it through. Unlike the demons it commanded, it didn't become a puff of smoke, but sank to the ground and slowly dissolved, dust taking its place and blowing away on the breeze.

I paused, looking out over the battle and seeing that many of the demons had hesitated. But not all of them. My group panted, some of them still fighting, and the other handler still commanded an army of shadow catchers and pushed them into battle.

I'd hoped it would have bought more relief. The dragons defending the city broke the line. While the gate guards and the dragons with equipment from the tunnels were still able to use charged weaponry, the rest were finding their shields and swords decaying under the rotten touch of the shadow catchers.

Although my mind could reach out that far, I couldn't connect to that much equipment that easily from so far away. I boosted them where I could and had to hope that it was enough.

As my group gathered more tightly around me again and I helped kill a couple of the more active shadow catchers, I bought them a little more breathing room.

"We need to take out the other handler," Jared said as he came closer. He was doing fairly well in battle for someone who, as far as I knew, wasn't used to fighting.

"Yup, but we've got to reach him first, and there's a lot

of trouble between us and him." I frowned, wondering if I had doomed us all. Although one handler was gone, the remaining one appeared to be stronger and more focused. He wasn't looking in our direction.

"Anything in that pack of yours that might help?" Flick pointed to the rucksack I never let out of my sight. I had shoved a bunch of things in it from the armory, though I hadn't tested a single one yet. But we were desperate, and if even one of them helped, it might be worth the few seconds to rummage and charge them.

I slipped back into the center of the group, grateful that Jared had stuck with us and given us an extra person to work with. Reaching into the pack, I found a ring and an amulet first.

Slipping the ring on, I lifted the amulet up and slung it over my head. I connected to both and tried to give them some of my energy. The ring seemed to reject it, but the amulet took some, and a thin sheen appeared across my entire body.

I had no idea what it did, but Neritas tried to reach out to take the thing and put it on himself. It stopped him, and a ripple of light flashing across my skin.

"Shield device of some kind?" he asked. I shrugged.

It seemed that way, but there was no guarantee it would protect me from a shadow catcher. Or anything that lurked in wait in the dark of night. Still not sure what the ring did, I pulled out another handful of items—a handheld device of some kind, a metal disk, and a brooch.

Powering the device seemed to wake it up, and its screen showed all the magic items around me like blips on a radar. I shoved it in a pocket and ignored it for now. The brooch took some energy, but not much, and then made me feel the strangest of feelings, as if I was struggling to remember something akin to an emotion.

Figuring that it wasn't going to be anything to help me in battle, I dropped it back into the top of my pack and charged the disk instead. Almost immediately it rose into the air, spinning and holding itself aloft. I raised an eyebrow, not sure what to do with it now. Carefully, I reached for it, plucking it from the air.

It let me move it as I wished, but as soon as I let go of it, it floated again. Testing it a little, I tried to gently spin it away from me, a bit like a frisbee. Ben caught it, smiling as he looked at it.

"I think I've seen one of these before. A long time ago. It's lethal if you target it right." Ben passed it back to me and I charged it some more, eager to test it out.

Wanting to get the hang of it, I first threw it at a shadow catcher that was a little way from us. It cut through the monster's neck and seemed to latch onto the demon, growing wider and thinner while it spun on the spot until it had cut the monster's head off.

As soon as the head came away, the creature died, puffing into smoke.

"Tell me you took more than one of those," Flick and Neritas said in unison.

I reached into the pack again and pulled out two more. Within seconds I had charged them somewhat and handed them one each.

"It's like watching kids in a candy store," Ben complained, but he was smirking as he said it. A moment later he was distracted by another shadow catcher coming in for a hit. Neritas killed it before Ben could do anything but block with his shield.

I steered our group in that direction. Flick threw his disk out as well to help clear the path and make it easier for us to get all three back.

When we had retrieved them and had a moment, I nodded toward the second handler.

"On three, we're all going to aim for that thing and hope one of us gets lucky."

They didn't need any extra encouragement as we all did so. The gap our previous kills had opened up was the only chance we were likely going to get. Neritas was the fastest to throw, then Flick, and finally me, aiming down the middle, between them. Flick's hit a shadow catcher that got in the way, and the handler noticed the one from Neritas and dodged it.

Neritas' lodged in another shadow catcher behind, drawing the handler's attention to it. Mine hit the handler in the back as Neritas and Flick were both attacked by demons closer to us.

The handler let out a high-pitched squeal as the small disk did its job, and for a moment the demons all hesitated. It allowed our group to move freely to get the disks back again to help finish off several more demons and give all the dragons fighting down in the dip between cliff and dragon city a brief reprieve.

"Let's finish it off." I raised my sword and charged toward the final handler.

I didn't need to encourage my group. We all let out battle cries and rushed it. Ben and Jace broke off to one side along the way as a stray shadow catcher took a sneaky stab toward us. Flick grabbed his disk again, slowing him, but Neritas was right beside me with the others behind us until we reached the handler.

He managed to break away from the disk and whirl back around as we got to him, but against all of us and caught off guard, he couldn't do much. Before he could draw one of those funky swords from its invisible sheath, I'd stabbed him once and Neritas stabbed him twice.

A moment later, Flick's disk flew past me and hit the handler. While he screeched and reeled in pain, we surrounded him and stabbed him multiple times. In seconds he was a crumpled heap on the ground, turning to dust.

We cheered as the shadow catchers all paused again, their minds no longer guided by a stronger, more capable demon. I grabbed my disk from the air as Flick and Neritas got theirs and we immediately threw them again, this time eager to cut a path back to the city and get back to helping the brave dragons defending it.

Now that they weren't being controlled, the shadow catchers started to think for themselves. In some cases that meant running away, but a lot of them still attacked the nearest dragon they could sniff out. Even without leaders, they were aggressive monsters and needed to be dealt with.

Thankfully no one was feeding them intelligence now, and that stopped them seeking out weaker dragons or aiming for wounds and injuries, and made them a little easier to kill. I also found that we could weave around some of them if they were already busy or distracted, allowing us to cut a path back to the city. As soon as I was in reach, I reconnected to all the dragons and the weapons they carried.

With their weapons charged back up, bravery returned to them all and the line straightened in defense of the city. Within a few more seconds we were absorbed back into it. My mother came over to me and hugged me as I noticed she sported another small injury. Capricia, Jace, Ben, and Jared had also gotten hurt, but nothing that was going to kill them, and my mom got to work healing them up right away.

Leaving her to it, I hurried back to the front line, taking over from those struggling the most and getting the stronger dragons to spread out. With the shadow catchers less organized, I encouraged everyone forward at the same pace, taking out any demons who hadn't run along the way.

No longer being forced by a handler to fight, some of them tried to flee when they were injured instead of letting themselves be killed. We threw disks at those ones. Flick and Neritas stuck with me and pushed on until we'd formed a V shape across the gap.

When there were fewer than ten shadow catchers left and we still hadn't stopped advancing, the remaining monsters seemed to pick up on their position, or another mind-controlling handler took over their control and made them all run away.

Other than throwing our disks one last time, I didn't let anyone follow or attack anymore, and we held the line for a few seconds before falling back to the city as well.

Somehow, we had done it. We had defended the city and killed a couple more handlers.

CHAPTER TWENTY-FIVE

My body ached from head to foot as I finally relaxed. I sheathed my sword and clipped my shield to my belt before I could drop them both, my arms heavy and tired. Neritas and Flick pocketed the disks I'd given them, making me grin.

When I turned to head back to the city, I saw Capricia give Sarai back her dagger, and I made a mental note to power it back up at the next good opportunity. I didn't do it now. The dragons around me were too tired for me to want to draw any more magic from them to power weapons. It could wait.

Now that the battle was over, I wasn't sure what would happen next. I had fought hard alongside people who had accused me of being in league with the demons and fought against that enemy. Surely now they could see that I wasn't lying and I wasn't serving the demons.

Despite my hopes, I didn't assume they would see the truth. I had gotten the feeling that Brenta didn't really want to know the truth. She'd been fighting whatever I did and said since the moment I had met her.

Once my mother had healed those who came to her for aid and anyone else she spotted, she came to be with me. Slowly my small army gathered up around and behind me again, with the addition of Jared, who had a proud light in his eyes and was still carrying the shiny charged equipment Merrik had given him.

The city guard was returning to the edge of the small parking lot, rejoining Capricia. I studied her body language as Brenta reappeared, no doubt having hidden during the fight.

"Thank you for your aid in defending the city." Capricia's voice was calm. I knew she was low on magic, but I prepared to fight her mood-altering abilities anyway, worried that if Brenta asked her to take control of her previous narrative in any way, I would struggle to calm things again.

"You're welcome. I will always defend anyone who needs it from these vile creatures. If nothing else, it seems to be something I have skills for."

"And it's something you've trained for. That much no one can doubt."

Her words said everything they needed to. She still doubted everything else.

"Will you allow Griffin to come up to the elders and show you what he's gathered? I don't have to come with him. I can stay here, but I think you'd benefit from hearing him out."

Although Capricia tilted her head to the side and

looked as if she might genuinely consider it, Brenta shook her head.

"Everything I said earlier stands. We believe you all to have been compromised by the enemy. Your hearts and minds have been corrupted and you would ask those of us who are safe to risk their lives for a cause that is unnecessary. I won't allow it in the city I care about."

I wanted to make a quip about her not caring about anything but her own agenda, but I felt Ben's hand on my shoulder.

"Come on, Scarlet. We cannot force the issue today. We'll find a way to prove that the city should be worried and do something about the demons and gate when the time is right."

I didn't like that this was the only option, but it was. There wasn't much else I could do right now. Griffin looked as if he might cry, but instead he shook his head.

"You used to be more open to discourse than this, Brenta. When did you get so set that you can't listen to an opposing viewpoint and find what is of merit within it? We're never going to entirely agree on everything, but making people leave your city because they believe something you aren't convinced is true... This is not the Brenta I've served beside for decades."

If Griffin's words got through to her, I couldn't tell. She turned and walked away before any of us could say anything else. Several other dragons went with her, but the guards remained, forming a less aggressive but still firm wall between us and the city.

Capricia stood in the center as she had before, and her body was still set.

"I hope everyone heals up and you can repair the damage." There was a lot of damage to both the guards under her command and the land around the city. Shadow catchers decayed everything they touched, and the land and cars had fared no better. I doubted all of the vehicles would work again. Thankfully most of ours had been protected and parked to one side, but one was looking worse for wear.

The road up to the top of the cliff wasn't too bad. Most of the shadow catchers had floated above it until they got caught in battle and thrashed around. It would let us drive away without too much trouble, but that was about all that was good for now.

When Jared didn't go with the others into the city or hand back what he'd gained, I went over to him.

"Don't say a word. I'm coming with you. If everyone in the city is too blind to see that you've just risked your life on yet another occasion to keep us all alive, then they're more stupid than I thought and don't deserve a flying teacher of my caliber. Besides, I miss adventure, and if I can have the opportunity to fly you into danger and see you and these crazy friends of yours come up with ways to defeat a bunch of demons, I'm all in."

As Jared spoke, the grin on my face grew wider and wider until I was almost laughing. It seemed I had another member in my team, and despite my fears, not everyone in the city had turned against me.

When I looked up at the city, I saw Tiffany standing on a bridge. She gave me a sad half-wave and I nodded back at her. She'd been one of my favorite classmates and I would be sorry to say goodbye to her as well, but she'd never been one to buck the trend or break the rules and I knew she would never dare to leave Detaris.

Everyone else in my little army gathered around by the cars.

"Some of us should return to the gate and the tunnels and keep the areas over there as secure as we can," Alitas said. "But I would wish to know where you are, Scarlet, so I can regularly see to your safety and report on the developments by the gate."

"I would also want that if I knew where I was going to go now."

"There's space at the farmhouse," Elias said. "And if that's not to your liking and you wish to be closer to the trouble, then the yacht you've been using can become a more permanent home. Though it will need some restocking and maintenance before it is completely suitable as a home."

"For now, the farmhouse works. Why doesn't everyone come with us there for tonight if there is space, sleep, and rest, and we can make longer term plans tomorrow."

It was a halfhearted suggestion. As much as I appreciated Elias and Sarai and wished to get to know them better, as well as Jace and the dragons she'd brought to fight beside me more than once, I felt as if I didn't have a home yet again.

With my mother also on the run with me, and now Ben having to walk away from the only home he'd ever known, I felt as if I was bringing chaos and pain to those around me. No one was immune to the pain of losing what mattered to them.

I tried not to worry about it as I got into the large van,

grateful Jace had brought it with her from the beginning. It meant that we all fit, even though one of the cars was bust and we'd gained an extra person.

Sitting between Neritas and Flick, I tried to decide whether I wanted to use the car journey to continue practicing my abilities. Should I even try? I didn't want to know how many demons were near a city I wouldn't be able to defend again in the future. If I knew how much danger lingered near them, I would worry and want to keep checking on them. This way I could let them fend for themselves and my mind wouldn't bother me.

Instead of doing anything productive, I tried to drift into sleep. I was exhausted and we had a long drive ahead of us.

Despite the tiredness, I couldn't quite get my mind to settle, and I was aware of all the conversation and movement around me. Nothing about this trip had gone the way I intended. Nothing had since the previous trip to find my mother. I had found her, but had not been prepared for everything that had followed.

A lot of others had been caught up in my madness, and I felt particularly sorry for dragons like Griffin and Flick, who had been doing what they felt was their duty and had lost everything they'd called home. Griffin had been trying to find answers on behalf of all the elders and they had rejected him.

On top of that, every single one of my friends risked their lives whenever they went anywhere with me. There were always shadow catchers, and it was always dangerous.

In the background I heard Ben talking with Jace and

Cios about the metal we'd found, the pillars, and what such a small group could do about the gate.

"Our group has some contacts who can help us gather information on that metal and the pillars, but it's going to take time. Until then, we should look at the way we all could be working together to power up the pillars that still work. Head over there as often as we can and put what we can in." Jace spoke quietly, but I was close enough I could still hear her.

"That was tough with the dragons we had last time. If the demons attack sooner, that could be a huge risk," Ben pointed out.

"We can charge up all the kit first. Make sure we can fight an entire battle without needing any more power."

"Did you see how many shadow catchers came at us today?" Cios asked his friend. "If they send even half as many, no amount of charged swords and shields are going to save us. We need more dragons before we can do anything. Scarlet is doing her best, but we need to help persuade dragons from some of the other cities to join us. The majority of Detaris may have decided to bury their heads in the sand, but not everyone did. Any dragons we can gain from other cities could help us turn the tide until we can fix the rest of the pillars."

They fell silent. There was nothing else to say. We could work on the problem, prepare for more trips to the gate, but the truth was that we had to work hard, find more allies and more knowledge, and it was all going to take time.

If the dragon world was united, we could have all

marched on the gate and done what we needed with what we had. Instead, we were going to have to try something else.

"Oh fuck," someone said a few seconds later.

I opened my eyes as everyone's attention was drawn to the dragon sitting near Jace. He had his phone in his hands and was watching a video. Within seconds we were all watching it.

Some people in the human world had been driving past when the shadow catchers and their handlers had attacked. They had a video of the demons marching up to the city, the shadow handlers heading in, revealing their true natures despite looking human moments before, and they disappeared behind this veil as well.

Not long after that they seemed to reappear, standing on an edge, visible, but not entirely. I watched in sick fascination as we appeared, flying on Jared, who turned into a human as we landed on the handler's position.

It was strange watching myself fight mere hours after it had happened, especially as I hadn't watched any of the videos of the previous fight. Seeing us work as an efficient team to kill so many of the shadow catchers had me feeling proud of us all.

On top of that, the viewers chimed in now and then, all of them having been terrified until they saw us fighting the creatures and killing them. They cheered us on, getting excited every time we killed another, and especially when I finished off a handler.

I watched as we paused for me to pull different devices from my bag and try them, and this confused our onlookers, but as soon as we stumbled upon the disks and went on our attack again they grew animated once more.

As we carved a path toward the other handler, the onlookers opted to get closer, zooming in a little and capturing better footage. It was at that moment they realized they recognized not only me but several of the others from our previous fight.

That was enough to make them move closer and continue cheering us on. It was a marvel that we hadn't heard them. Their screams of encouragement sounded so loud on the video, but they had been on the other side of the road at the top of the cliff and careful to avoid the shadow catchers as they continued to arrive.

A couple of times, the creatures came right past them, summoned by the handlers to attack us, and the humans got close-up footage. I shuddered at the monstrosities. They called them demons and monsters as well.

The video ended not long after we defeated the second handler and headed back to the city and through the veil that surrounded it to finish off the last of the shadow catchers. Not wanting to get caught up in the chaos as other demons near them were cut loose mentally, and aware they were unlikely to see anything else, the humans chose self-preservation at that point and drove away.

Griffin shook his head. "That's not going to go down well with the other elders. Not when that's out there along with the previous video."

"I get the feeling that dragons won't be able to hide from this world much longer," I mused. "If we continue to fight the shadow catchers and are going to keep trekking to the gate, we're going to attract more attention.

Remember that group of humans we ran into the first time?"

Alitas nodded his head and sighed.

"They will talk now if they see this or the previous video. We are going to have to look out for humans as well as demons from now on." Ben frowned as the group fell silent.

Although I knew it might not help, I couldn't entirely share in the disheartened state of everyone around me. Hiding from humanity was never going to work long term. Magic only hid a group for so long when everyone had the ability to make a video and share it with the whole world. It changed everything, to be able to keep making videos and putting them out for the world to see and analyze.

There were going to be plenty of people who assumed it was a hoax, but the more times we were caught on camera, the more people were going to believe and question and be curious.

I hoped that when the veil was finally lifted, we would be understood and accepted. And not feared or misjudged.

Either way, I couldn't worry about it right now. We still needed to solve the problem of where we were all going to go long term and how I was going to start the effort to see the gate and its defenses repaired, reinstalled, and charged back up again. No small task when I had nothing but the pack on my back and the items in my pockets and hanging from my belt.

Seeing the farmhouse looking warm and inviting in the evening breeze helped calm my anxiety, at least for now. Elias and Sarai were opening their home to us and helping us get back on our feet. Whether I would be safe there long term was another matter.

I went inside to find more familiar faces and a decent meal that helped me relax more. I sat in the large kitchen at the solid wooden table with a bowl full of stew and comrades in arms around me while everyone rested. A part of me already felt at home, but I knew this was a haven for a lot of dragons who wanted to fly under the radar. They didn't all want someone like me around, especially when I came with so much attention and trouble.

When we'd all finished eating and the conversation had died down, the nearest dragon leaned closer to me.

"What are you going to do? Looks like you've got a kingdom that needs showing a tough hand or two." The dragon smiled as if he liked the idea of bringing them to recognize my authority. I didn't like the tone of the question and didn't know how to respond.

Elias stepped in. "Now, now. We'll not have any of that kind of talk. Not only are we not going to encourage forcing any dragon to do anything—after all, most of us are here because we don't like being told what to think—but now is not the time to talk of the future. Most of the dragons here have just lost their homes and have fought a long battle against darkness. Let them rest and decide what they wish to do without the outside influence of another." He spoke gently, but everyone listened, and I got the feeling that he knew they would.

It ended the conversation before it began and made it clear we would be welcome to stick around until we'd figured ourselves out. For now, that was enough.

Being a queen wasn't something I'd wanted to become,

and the weight was off my shoulders now that I didn't need to be. But the knowledge I had and the responsibility to act on it hadn't gone away. In some ways my task was now easier. I didn't have to stand on a pedestal for anyone, just find the right dragons to help protect the world.

EPILOGUE

Looking out across the water, I tried not to let the unease get to me. I felt shadow catchers rotating slowly around the lake and the yacht in the center of it. I stood on the deck, watching the sun set on another strange day.

After staying at the farmhouse for a few days, I and most of the dragons close to me had opted to come to the yacht. It was safer out here. My mother, Reijo, Ben, Neritas, and Flick were sticking to me like glue. The honor guards I had gained, headed by Alitas and Kryos, continued to come and go, focusing on what they felt was their duty in protecting me and keeping an eye on the gate for me.

On top of that, Jace had visited almost every single day, determined to get me the information I needed to repair the gate and its pillars as well as get a feel for the acceptance I might get in other cities.

The rest of the time I had been practicing my abilities, strengthening them, learning to do everything I needed more efficiently and fighting shadow catchers.

After a week of intensive training and practice, I could

feel the constant circle of shadow catchers around the lake and work out how many were out there. If a handler was guiding them, I couldn't tell from where, and I didn't know if they could feel me or not, but they were slowly circling my position.

Every evening I also spent a few minutes checking the social media in the human world. I had been recognized as the person in the videos and someone had dredged up my name and backstory. An orphan who now seemed to be a magical warrior fighting demons. And that meant the few friends I had from before I'd discovered I was a dragon also knew.

That information had got to my old boss, and they were all trying to contact me. I hadn't responded to any of them yet. I couldn't decide if I really wanted to. If the dragon world had been hiding for so many millennia, it didn't feel right for me to be the one to blow it wide open. And I knew that if I replied to my friends or boss, one of them would talk.

For now, the phone I had was off, in the bottom of a pack that Alitas had hidden somewhere in the forest. If I wanted it back, he'd get it for me, but for now, it was unfindable and most importantly, no one could get to me.

Now that I could feel the shadow catchers, my group of dragons and I had hunted them a couple of times and fought them. It was good practice, helped us work out the equipment we'd gained, and made me more confident about leading a larger group across to the gate again, but we weren't there or ready for that yet.

When the sun had slipped below the horizon and I was starting to feel cold, I noticed the telltale glint of a car coming up the track to the lake. In case of emergencies, a motorboat was tethered up by the yacht and another on the shore, so whoever it was would be able to come straight to me, but I hadn't been expecting any more visitors today.

Jace pulled up, a smile on her face as Jared got out with her. A moment later Alitas appeared, coming out from behind the small hut we'd had put on the shore for the guards.

They quickly got into the motorboat on the shore and headed my way to join me on the yacht. I watched them come over, trying to ignore the chill in the air.

Flick and Neritas came to see where I was before Jace reached us, but they heard the noise of the motor and helped her tether and climb aboard.

Jace looked me over. "I could do with a drink, Red. I've just driven a very long way."

I grinned and invited them all below deck for dinner and drinks. Although it was good to see them, I hadn't been expecting Jace today and I was surprised she was here.

"Thought I'd bring you some good news," she said as soon as she sat. Neritas poured her a whiskey while Flick got Jared a drink and Ben went to let everyone else know we had visitors and were going to have dinner soon.

"I could do with good news."

"We managed to get into contact with some dragons we used to know. Asked them to spread the word about what's going on here."

"I've got some friends I used to fly with in Utah," Jared added.

"And Cios knows two of their city guards. Used to study with them. Or get up to mischief, more like."

"Is that where you were?" I felt a zip of excitement course through my body.

Jace nodded. "They want to know more, and they're not committed, but their response is positive. Their city doesn't hate the idea of a red dragon and they don't think you are a pretentious bitch before they even meet you."

I'd have chuckled had it not still stung that the dragons in Detaris didn't like me for simply being red, but either way, I was grateful they'd come to tell me. It had done what they intended—lifted my mood and given me some hope again.

Sharing a meal with so many of my friends helped to improve my mood until I was sitting back with a glass of wine in hand, grateful that although things hadn't gone to plan lately, I wasn't alone, and I wasn't out of options.

I might not have been a queen, and I wasn't a savior, but I was able to keep doing what mattered and work with my friends and use my abilities to protect the world, and that was enough for now.

THE STORY CONTINUES

The story continues with book five, *Dragon Defying*, available at Amazon.

Claim your copy today!

ACKNOWLEDGMENTS

When I plotted this series at the end of 2021, I did so with the thought that I would knock all of them out in 2022 and they would be published mostly in the same year. You, my darling readers have been so enthusiastic about my dragon books that I hoped to give you a series a year of more of the stuff you loved and keep taking you on the many dragon adventures I've got in my head, but to say the year didn't go to plan would be an understatement.

I think, however, that the books are better for having been delayed. I've grown as a person a lot this last year and I'd like to think that it's also reflected in my writing and where the stories and characters are at. I'd hope that you've been given a better experience for the delay and if nothing else, I'm now very grateful when I get to sit down for several days and immerse myself in the wonder of my writing worlds.

This also leads me to a huge thank you to everyone at LMBPN for everything they do, especially Robin, Steve, Kelly, Grace, Tracey and Jacqui. You're all superstars who have held my year together and helped me keep everything moving and the books flowing as best as possible. I am blessed to be one of your authors.

To Bryan, for so much that I struggle to put into words, but for being the constant encouragement, for believing I can do anything I set my mind to, for encouraging me to be myself, and for opening my eyes to what it feels like to be truly loved and cared for.

To my tiny humans, for giving me something to strive for and teaching me so much about who I am in your own way. You have a way of making me see the world that I'd never have gained without you and I love having you in my life. Our future adventures might not include dragons, but they are going to be epic.

To Bear, Andrew, David, Clare and Anne-Mhairi. You folks rock and we really need to all have a holiday together sometime. With any luck the books and creative endeavors of all of us will pay for it soon.

And to God. You've got this. And it means everything to see that and know that in my life.

ABOUT THE AUTHOR

Jess is in the process of changing her name. She's been through a difficult year that leaves her wanting a fresh start and a chance to be the person she's always meant to be. Over the next little while all her books will be moving to Talia Beckett and you'll find all future releases under this author name.

Talia was born in the quaint village of Woodbridge in the UK, has spent some of her childhood in the States and now resides near the beautiful Roman city of Bath. She lives with her two tiny humans (one boy and one girl) and near an amazing group of friends who support her career and life choices.

During her still relatively short life Talia has displayed an innate curiosity for learning new things and has therefore studied many subjects, from maths and the sciences, to history and drama. Talia now works full time as a writer and mummy, incorporating many of the subjects she has an interest in within her plots and characters.

When she's not busy with work and keeping her tiny humans alive she can often be found with friends, playing with miniature characters, dice and pieces of paper covered in funny stats and notes about fictional adventures her figures have been on.

You can find out more about the author and her

upcoming projects by joining her on facebook, by watching her live D&D streams, or emailing her via books@jessmountifield.co.uk. Talia loves hearing from a happy fan so please do get in touch!

Talia is also opening up her discord for fans to come chat about what she's up to, and see a few sneak peaks of future work. There's also a chance to become one of her beta readers. If you'd like to check that out you can do so here.

CONNECT WITH THE AUTHOR

Connect with Talia

Mailing list sign up
Facebook group.
Discord group
Actual play D&D stream: Twitch or Youtube
Email address: contact me here.

BOOKS BY JESS MOUNTIFIELD / TALIA BECKETT

Already published

Urban Fantasy

Dragon of Shadow and Air:

Air Bound

Shadow Sworn

Dragon Souled

Earth Bound

Night Sworn

Dryad Souled

Water Bound

Day Sworn

Pegasus Souled

Fire Bound

Light Sworn

Phoenix Souled

Dragon Apparent:

Dragon Missing

Dragon Seeking

Dragon Revealed

Dragon Rising

Time of the Dragon (with Andrew Bellingham):

Dragon's Code

Dragon's Inquisition

Dragon's Redemption

Fantasy

Tales of Ethanar:

Wandering to Belong (Tale 1)

Innocent Hearts (Tale 2 & 3)

For Such a Time as This (Tale 4)

A Fire's Sacrifice (Tale 5)

Winter Series:

The Hope of Winter (Tale 6.05)

The Fire of Winter (Tale 6.1)

Guild of the Eternal Flame:

Wayfarer's Sanctuary

Protector's Secret

Healer's Oath

Other Fantasy:

The Initiate (under Holly Lujah)

Writing with Dawn Chapman:

Jessica's Challenge (#5 in the Puatera Online series)
Dahlia's Shadow (#6 in the Puatera Online series)
Lila's Revenge (#7 in the Puatera Online series)

Sci-Fi:
Fringe Colonies:

Alliance

Haven

Rebellion

Rebirth

Reclamation

Star Trail:

Hunted

Sherdan series:

Sherdan's Prophecy

Sherdan's Legacy

Sherdan's Country

Sherdan's Road (A short story in the anthology 'The End of the Road')

The Slave Who'd Never Been Kissed (A short in the charity anthology 'Imaginings')

New Beginnings

Santa's Little Space Pirate

In the multi-author Adamanta series:

Episode 1 – Adamanta

Episode 3 – Excelsior

Episode 8 – Phoenix

Episode 13 – New Contacts

Episode 17 – Sacrifice

Other:

Clues, Claws and Christmas

Non-Fic:

How to Write Lots, and Get Sh*t Done: the Art of Not Being a Flake

Find purchase links here

Coming soon:

Urban Fantasy:

Dragon Apparent:

Dragon Defying

Dragon Crowned

Dragon Defending

Time of the Dragon (with Andrew Bellingham):

Dragon's Revolt

Dragon's Summit

Fantasy:

(Tales of Ethanar):

The Pursuit of Winter (#2 in the Winter series, Tale 6.2)

Books under Amelia Price

Mycroft Holmes Adventures:

The Hundred Year Wait

The Unexpected Coincidence

The Invisible Amateur

The Female Charm

The Reluctant Knight

The Ambitious Orphan

The Unconventional Honeymoon Gift

The Family Reunion

The Immortal Problem

The Unremarkable Assistant

Coming soon:

Mycroft 11

OTHER BOOKS FROM LMBPN
PUBLISHING

Sign up for the LMBPN email list to be notified of new releases and special deals!

https://lmbpn.com/email/

For a complete list of books by LMBPN please visit:

https://lmbpn.com/books-by-lmbpn-publishing/

www.ingramcontent.com/pod-product-compliance
Lightning Source LLC
LaVergne TN
LVHW041754060526
838201LV00046B/998